I Can Make Out With Any Girl Here

D1501987

I Can Make Out With Any Girl Here

By

Ryan Nemeth

Cover Art by Erin Murphy

YELLOW SNOW
An Imprint of *Diversion Press, Inc.*

ISBN 978-1-935290-03-2 (alk. paper)
Library of Congress Control Number: 2009926672

Published by Yellow Snow, an imprint of Diversion Press, Inc.
Clarksville, Tennessee
www.diversionpress.com

Acknowledgments

Don Nemeth, Kelly Nemeth, Nick Nemeth and Donny Nemeth. Diversion Press, for giving the story a look. Diversion Press, for then reconsidering months later and deciding to give the story a second look. Jonny, Jannik, Bryan, Kim, Q-Tip, Lauren, Shawn, Carolyn, Jimmy the Rocket, Eddie, and Pete, for reading the original drafts. Molly, who let me do a lot of revising at her house. Former inhabitants of Brockman Hall (2-South), including James, Greg, Pete, Fargo, Sam, Steve, Bones, Jeff, Nick, Christian, Josh, Adam, the other Nick, and Eve. The 2003-2007 Xavier University Rugby Team. *Barely Legal Teens* (at the time of this printing, the longest-running improv comedy show in the history of Cincinnati, Ohio): Ted, Dan, Molly, Natalie, Farsad, Monica, Alison, Katrina, Bradd, Paul, and Bill. Paul Barker, Greg Urbas and Saint Edward High School. Al Franken, whose *Why Not Me?* was a great inspiration. Beven, who, many years ago, unknowingly helped me title this book. Me, whose vision, dedication, courage and unique (yet marketable) sense of humor made this project possible in the first place. And, finally, that poor fetal pig, who triumphantly chose to give every one of his nine lives so that his tale would live on forever in book form.

To Gizmo and Jack the Dog

Application Essay

I feel that over the last four years enrolled at Blairmont High I have grown as a person, as a citizen of this great country of ours, and most importantly, **as a student.** To continue to grow I feel it is necessary to enrich myself with a culturally diverse college experience. My family feels and I feel as well that Kulhman University would be a great place for me to flourish both academically and socially (as well as culturally). And if time and circumstance allow I feel I should also grow spiritually.

Kulhman University (the famed "glove-box of the Midwest") has a lot to offer in the area of diversity. My high school has an all-male student body so I feel it is necessary for me to experience what it is like to live, work and learn with students who are both female as well as male at the same time. Kulhman University offers students of all genders rich learning opportunities. I strongly feel that for this reason alone Kulhman University would be a great fit for my strong feelings (and even stronger emotions) on diversity.

Though I do not yet know what I feel I want to major in, this does not mean that I am not prepared for the life of being a college student. Whichever field I choose to concentrate in will (I feel) be both an informed decision on my part and also on the part of the tremendous guidance and advising staff that is part of Kulhman University's **rich and tremendous** tradition. (As of right now, I feel that I favor either Accounting or Art History as my top two choices. Though it has come to my attention that Kulhman University does not offer either an Accounting or an Art History major, even that will not stop me from applying to this tremendous university.)

1

Having discussed my college decision with my family (as well as with my own mind and feelings) I am confident and proud of my saying that Kulhman University is my **first choice of school to attend.** I feel that if I were to be accepted to your tremendous school that my emotions would be greater than when I first learned to ride a bike all those proud years ago. I am also prepared to **abandon my current girlfriend** in order to expand my ever-expanding and maturing horizon(s) in the rich and tremendous campus life of such a university as rich and tremendous as Kulhman University. Thank you for considering my application.

Donald Blake
Blairmont High

Kuhlman University
Office of Admissions
2900 Salvage Parkway
Tomaschevske, OH 46121

Dear Donald,

Hopefully the college application process is winding down and you have a chance to relax and enjoy what's left of senior year.

As you know, Kulhman University (the famed "Glove-box of the Midwest") has a *rich and tremendous* tradition. As you may not know, this year we received over 15,000 applications for admission for Fall Semester 2007. That is a record-setting number of applicants for Kulhman. I'm sure you can imagine this makes the jobs of our admissions staff both trying and stressful (*very* trying and *very* stressful).

While we are sure that your test scores and high school transcripts make you a qualified candidate for Kulhman University, we simply cannot accommodate every single applicant. With well over 15,000 applications to evaluate it is inevitable that great prospects (great prospects such as yourself!) will slip through the cracks. This year, with so many applications (15,000+) we simply didn't have time to open all (more than 15,000) envelopes. Perhaps we will get around to them, but it is doubtful. As you may have guessed because you are receiving this letter, we did get around to yours.

Again, it is with regret (great regret) that we inform you that not all 15,000 applicants can be chosen for admission for this upcoming Fall Semester. 15,000 is a huge number! A small, private school such as Kulhman University could not physically contain that large (15,000) a freshman class.

3

Many applicants who were not accepted choose to wait a semester and apply again after retaking the SAT and ACT tests. Other rejected applicants decide to attend another university, college, or trade school. Still others never open their rejection letters and blindly assume they were accepted. Much to the dismay of our faculty, staff, and accepted students, these idiot *non-students* often stupidly arrive on campus at the start of the Fall Semester and are very confused and shocked when they do not find a dorm room assigned to them.

With that said, we are proud to welcome you into Kulhman University's *rich and tremendous* tradition. You have been accepted for the Fall Semester 2007, Class of 2011. Congratulations on your acceptance. An admissions packet including dormitory and roommate assignment will arrive within a few weeks.

Sincerely,

Alice Closser

Kulhman University Office of Admissions

My Freshman Year at Kulhman University

Donny Blake

PRIVATE! DO NOT READ!

August 25

It was a long (five hours) drive but it was worth it—I just moved into my dorm at Kuhlman University. I am a college student! Parents left at 3 o'clock. Busy meeting new "hall mates"—I'll write more later!

August 25

"Hall mates" are a diverse group. Roommate ("James") seems to be really shy and concerned about meeting new people. Confided to me that he is from rural area and has hard time opening up in new situations and that first day at college is big culture shock for him. Thought he might turn out to be a real pussy if I didn't do something fast, so I took it upon myself to lighten the mood. I jokingly told him to treat his first day at college like his first day in prison and that he should beat somebody up right away to make a name for himself. We had a good laugh about how could a small guy like him ever beat somebody up LOL. Also pointed out that no one would be scared of a "dork" or "pointdexter" like him because he wears glasses. He seemed to enjoy my goofing around, so went on to say that at least he didn't have to be nervous about talking to girls because what girl would be caught dead talking to loser like him.

August 25

    James has good punching abilities. Left room for while. Went around meeting people in hall. Here is a rundown of hallmates in my wing (Second Floor, South):

James: Roommate. Looks like nerd. Punches like gang member. No sense of humor.

Peter: From New York. Friendly. Gave him cool nickname ("New York Pete").

Mike: Tall. From New Jersey. Has lots of snacks in room. Also gave him cool nickname ("Jersey"). Is New York Pete's roommate.

Andrew: Funny. From Fargo, North Dakota. Wears strange black leather sandals and is unusually flexible. Can bend his hand almost all the way backward! Have given him cool nickname of "Fargo" (in spite of strange sandals and strange hand-flexibility).

Bryan: Quiet. Pretty nondescript so far. Roommate of Fargo.

Kyle: Has no roommate and not surprising because he is WEIRD. Smells of sweat and old people. Pushy. Talks a lot. From Los Angeles (**Will not get cool nickname from me because of smell and weirdness).

Jeff: Loves God. A lot.

Adam: Loves having sex with his girlfriend. A lot. Loves having sex with his girlfriend probably as much as Jeff loves God. This causes some friction between Jeff and Adam, who happen to be roommates, as Jeff claims that premarital sex is sinful and will lead to an eternity of damnation. I don't think these roommates are off to a great start, but at least they address their differences with words and not violence (unlike my dickhead roommate James who is a dickhead).

Nick: Asian (short). Has cool Jeep. Also has temper. Does not actually live in dorm.

Kenny: Resident Assistant (RA). Upperclassmen. In charge of hall. Talks with lisp. Lives by himself.

8

Steve & Steven: Two guys with same name at end of hall. Steve is slightly shorter one. Both Steve and Steven (tall) play guitar. Could get annoying.

Donny: (me) (cool guy)

August 26

Went out with New York Pete and Jersey last night. Checked out popular student bar called SUNSETS. Four-dollar pitchers: good. Dance floor: also good. Got close look at female student body (pun). *Seriously, though, there doesn't seem to be many good-looking girls who go to KU.*

Met girl named Jen who was world-class dork. Very ugly plus very bad personality. We tried to avoid her but she followed us around everywhere and even waited for us when we went to the bathroom.

Competed in pitcher-drinking race with New York Pete as teammate. Took seventh place: not bad. Ugly Jen, who clearly had no other friends, cheered us on. How sad!

Felt bad for lonely, Ugly Jen so had sex with her to make her feel better. Think it worked.

This morning I didn't want to talk to her so I pretended to be in a really deep sleep so she would leave on her own. At first it was easy to pretend to be asleep. But as the hours dragged on it became harder and harder and she for some reason kept cuddling with my (seemingly) lifeless body. It became increasingly difficult to pretend to sleep when our dorm decided to test the fire alarms and Jen thought it was a real fire and carried my "sleeping" body out of bed, down the hallway, down a flight of stairs and out the front door. She is very strong. All the while I pretended to be asleep and I guess Ugly Jen thought she saved my life. I should have gotten as Oscar!

KU CAMPUS POLICE NOTES FOR THE WEEK OF
8/20 – 8/26

Sunday, August 25 4:05pm

During a routine fire alarm testing in Montgomery Hall, most freshman residents evacuated in a timely fashion. One unconscious resident, however, failed to hear both the alarms as well as the clatter of his fellow students exiting the building. The subject was heroically dragged out of the building by another student. The unconscious student slept through the entire ordeal, as well as a full physical examination by Kulhman Health Services staff. The subject was found to be in good health and determined to be medically asleep. When the subject finally awoke, a KU Campus Police officer briefed him on fire safety and gave him extensive literature on fire and tornado protocol. He was also given handouts on sleep-related medical ailments, courtesy of the Health Services staff. The subject was not fined.

August 27

    First day of classes. Have cute French professor, Madame Bierbaum-Cardeaux. Anything to look at besides Ugly Jen's ugly face.

August 27

    Bad idea having sex with Ugly Jen Saturday night because now she knows which room I live in. I am very sorry to report that earlier in the evening Ugly Jen showed up at my room for more ugly sex with me. I am getting the feeling (and both New York Pete and Jersey agree with me) that just because she saved my life from non-existent fire and that we have had sex twice that Ugly Jen thinks we are friends now. Get a life! P.S. Even asshole roommate James thinks Ugly Jen is ugly.

August 29

    Week halfway over. Classes okay so far. Told Ugly Jen that we are through. My first college break-up! Celebrated with New York Pete and Asian Nick (who we now call Ninja Nick because of his ultra Asian-ness). The three of us hung out in New York Pete's room and drank vodka that Ninja Nick bought from a gas station. We talked about how ugly Ugly Jen was. She was so ugly!

August 30

Bringing up all those memories about Ugly Jen really got me thinking that I was too hard on her yesterday. So after New York Pete and Ninja Nick fell asleep I called her to apologize. She ended up coming over for sex on New York Pete's floor. Bad move, Donny!

Also, Kenny the RA saw Ugly Jen leaving this morning but didn't write me up for having a girl over because he thought she was a boy (this was both good *and* bad).

August 31

Classes over for the week.

Ninja Nick set-up my computer for me. Asian or not, Ninja Nick is really good with electronics.

This weekend there is a big street-wide party on Hudson Avenue called HudsonFest. Have avoided Ugly Jen since Wednesday night's "mistake" and am looking forward to meeting new people at HudsonFest! See ya Sunday!

September 2

HudsonFest was awesome until Ugly Jen showed up. We ended up having sex in a basement of one of the houses and I guess she thought that we were back together or something (I guess she's both ugly *and* stupid) so I had to re-break-up with her.

Most of my hallmates came out to HudsonFest. It was interesting to see them off campus. Both Fargo and Bryan came and seemed to have a great time. Fargo was a big hit with the upperclassmen due to his double-jointed hand-bending tricks he does. Steve and Steven came, and ended up puking all over the place. Lightweights! Adam and I hit it off. We joked around about our roommate problems together. Until my roommate James showed up and I decided to hide in bathroom for a bit.

Will write more tomorrow. (Am hungover and exhausted.)

September 3

(Am still hungover and exhausted.)

September 5

Feeling slightly better. Decided to go to SUNSETS with Adam, Ninja Nick and New York Pete. A lot of other guys from my hallway either A) Didn't want to go, B) Don't have fake IDs and can't get in to bars, or C) Weren't invited (i.e., my dickhead roommate James).

Luckily my cousin gave me his ID the week before I left for college. Though it is cracked, expired and says I am six-foot-three (I am five-foot-eleven with shoes on) it vaguely looks like me and that seems to be enough for a place like SUNSETS.

More crowded than last week. Danced with a few girls. Had fun.

Saw Ugly Jen dancing with other guy who was equally as ugly as she. Wanted to go over and thank guy for taking her off my hands. He's in for a treat, heh heh! Damn, she is ugly! They're so ugly together that it's hilarious! Ninja Nick asked if it bothered me to see Ugly Jen dancing with other dude. Said no way, why would I care?

OUTBOX
Sep 6, 1:14AM
To: UGLYJEN

I CAN'T BELIEVE YOU WOULD DO THAT RITE IN FRONT
OF ME. I THOUGHT I MEANT SOMETHING TO U. GOODBYE
4EVR, JEN.

OUTBOX
Sep 6, 1:15AM
To: UGLYJEN

THAT GUY IS AN AWESOME DANCER. I NEVER WANT TO
TALK TO YOU AGAIN. I HATE U. I LOVE U.

September 6

Ended up having sex with stupid Ugly Jen last night. Stupid, stupid, stupid!

September 9

Decided to "go home" for weekend. (I actually didn't go home, I just told that to Ugly Jen so she'd leave me alone.) In reality I went to the zoo on Saturday with New York Pete and Fargo. Got to feed colorful birds. Found out that Fargo is scared of bats—may or may not be useful information later on.

We all went to a party later that night where I drunkenly made out with not one but two girls. They were both normal looking and not ugly or mannish like hideously sicko Ugly Jen. Didn't get their numbers or names, was too drunk. Doesn't matter—there'll be more. I'm back, baby!

September 10

Spirits are so high that I decided to try making nice with my roommate James. Found out that though he is from Texas he is huge Yankees fan. Showed me souvenir bat autographed by Derek Jeter he bought on eBay. Though I was almost positive it was phony I didn't say anything for fear of getting hit with fake autographed bat (which would undoubtedly hurt as badly as genuine bat would). We are making progress. Classes are fine. Think I will write love note to Madame Bierbaum-Cardeaux to express my affection.

September 10

Reconsidered plan of writing love note to Madame Bierbaum-Cardeaux. Decided to play it cool instead. Have not heard from Ugly Jen.

September 13

Party tonight. Will go with Adam and New York Pete. Decided to invite James along. Staying true to his usual dickhead demeanor, he refused, saying he would rather "get fucked by a homeless dog" than hang out with me in public. Also, I think he is stealing my Pop Tarts. I feel bad for James, because someday his attitude is going to get him in trouble.

Kuhlman University

2900 Salvage Parkway
Tomaschevske, OH 46121

RE: Two-South Washroom

Dear Resident:

Last night a window in the two-south washroom was broken. Next to the shards of shattered glass was a baseball bat, which seems to be marked with a poorly faked autograph of popular Yankees shortstop Derek Jeter, though it looks more like "Derbik Jester" or "Debbie Jemstone." The (dry-erase?) marker used to pen the phony autograph has been somewhat blurred due to the fact that the bat was apparently urinated on excessively after the window was broken.

Whether this was an accident, a senseless act of vandalism, or a politically motivated attack on Mr. Jeter's character is not my concern. My concern is that this window gets paid for and replaced. Someone in this hallway is responsible. I have been an RA for two years now and I know how to handle this type of situation: by scotch-taping notes like this to your doors.

The cost of the window is $45.00 and if someone does not come forward by the end of the week the entire hallway will be forced to split the cost.

*If the guilty party would like to remain anonymous, he (she?) may slip a note under my door and we can take care of this discreetly. Though I doubt that will happen since you freshmen love to brag about how you drunkenly break (and urinate on) other peoples' property, please at least consider that possibility.

Thank you,
Kenny
ex. 4499

September 14

Have been avoiding James all day. I think he knows I "borrowed" his phony autographed bat last night. Unless he decided to pour garbage all over my mattress for another reason. Need to raise $45 <u>fast</u>.

September 15

Decided to go home for weekend (really go home, not fake "go home" like last weekend). Ninja Nick let me borrow his Jeep to drive back. He said I could use it but I owe him **two favors** (??). Good to be home. Mom happy to see me. Shih Tzu Samuel also happy to see me. Dad confused as to why I am home and not at school.

September 15

I am going over Keelie's house to watch a movie (*Kicking and Screaming* starring Will Ferrell). I should note that Keelie is my "real girlfriend" from home. When she asked what college was like so far I wanted to tell her how ugly some of the girls were, specifically Ugly Jen, but then I thought that might not be the best idea. Since Keelie is my girlfriend don't think it is wise to mention Ugly Jen. Should also note that Keelie is a junior in high school.

20

September 15

I feel that I should point out that Keelie and I have never had sex. This is because I'm not a weirdo and would not have physical relations because I am a freshman in college and she is in high school and she is very smart and great and someone I respect immensely. Plus she's extremely prude for a sixteen year-old.

September 16

I must have dozed off and talked in sleep during *Kicking and Screaming* starring Will Ferrell because when I woke up Keelie was sitting on opposite side of couch with very angry expression on face saying, "You dozed off and talked in sleep during *Kicking and Screaming* starring Will Ferrell." Apparently I kept saying the words 'Ugly Jen' over and over again and sucking my thumb. I panicked when she told me this. But then I managed to convince her that 'Ugly Jen' is the nickname of a ghost that haunts one of the dorms at Kulhman. She bought it!

Still no sex, ~~unfortunately~~, which is good because Keelie is too young to do that type of thing. Way too young. And innocent. Innocent and pure. ~~And tender.~~ *I am not a weirdo.*

21

September 17

Back at school. Ninja Nick pleased that Jeep is returned safely and reminded me that I owe him two favors. Still would not explain what that means. Is maybe Asian custom?

Paid Kenny the $45 for broken bathroom window. That should keep James off my back. Got money from Keelie who thinks it is for Ghost Hunter fees to rid dorm of evil spirits. Hahaha.

Seriously, though, I feel guilty for taking money from her for supposed Ghost Hunter fees. I don't like lying to her. I also feel guilty for all the cheating on her I've been doing (with Ugly you-know-who). But my guilt is balanced by the good feelings I have for not having sex with her because she is sixteen. Decided that the good outweighs the bad in this situation, and that I am a great guy!

September 17

Weird, smelly Kyle needed help moving a couch into his room so I helped him even though he is weird and smelly. This only confirms what a great guy I am!

September 17

Stopped by Jersey's room to see how his
weekend was. Really, though, I just wanted
some of his snacks. He has tons of junk food
in there. He gave me a bag of Cheez-Its. Never
had those before. Not bad. Really cheesy.

September 19

The guys wanted to go out to SUNSETS for
a few drinks. I wasn't so sure I should go,
though, because I'm short on cash. Everyone
was drinking in New York Pete and Jersey's
room before they left so I hung out with them
for a while. Mainly so I could eat another bag
of Cheez-Its. The cheesy flavor is unlike
anything I've ever had. It tastes like real
cheese. Amazing.

September 20

Good thing I didn't go out last night. I
checked my balance with my debit card today. I
only have nine bucks in my account. Well, now
seven, because it charged me to check my
balance.

```
----------------------------------------
            KULHMAN BOOKSTORE ATM
----------------------------------------
    TERMINAL #          = D303421
    DATE                = 09/20/2007

    CARD NUMBER         = XXXXXXXXXXXX4454

    DISPENSED AMOUNT    = 00.00
    REQUESTED AMOUNT    = 00.00
    FROM ACCOUNT          checking

    TERMINAL FEE        = 2.00
    ORIGINAL BALANCE    = 9.31
    TOTAL AMOUNT        = 2.00

    CURRENT BALANCE     = 7.31

----------------------------------------
```

September 21

Really had craving for Cheez-Its today. Almost used my debit card to buy some from the bookstore, but reminded myself that I can't spend money because of seven dollar bank account balance.

P.S. Think it might be worth it to get into banking trouble over these things because they are so damn cheesy.

Not enough comes in the package, though, because I always want more! Found old Cheez-Its wrapper in garbage and licked crumbs from inside of it.

September 21

There are a few parties tonight but I told the guys that I might stay in.

***I think Jersey has a few more bags of Cheez-Its in his closet.

September 22

Stayed in last night. Basically I hung out in New York Pete and Jersey's room all night eating Cheez-Its. I fell asleep in Jersey's bed. I think he was pissed because when I woke up he was cleaning up all the Cheez-Its wrappers really loudly like making a big show of it and I'm like okay, I get it you're mad that I ate your food, get over it already.

Oh, I almost forgot! I got a call from Ugly Jen last night but I didn't pick up. She left a message. Said something about how she got my drunk-dial message last weekend? But I don't remember calling her. She's probably lying. Whatever.

**Transcript of voice message left on
mobile phone of JENNIFER SHAPIRO on
Saturday September 14 at 3:34 AM:**

Jen. Jen, pick up. Jen, it's me. Listen,
I know you're mad but just pick up.
Please I wanna talk to you. Hey, Ninja,
gimme another beer. Jen?

[SOUND OF CAN BEING OPENED]

Jen? This beer is warm. Jen, I know you
can hear me. Just pick up. What?

[INAUDIBLE]

Yes, she can hear me. Did you microwave
this beer or something? Yes, I know it's
a cell phone, Adam. Dude, I'm leaving a
message. I know she can hear me. She
just won't pick up 'cuz she's pissed at
me and she's being a bitch. Sorry Jen I
didn't mean that. I just called to tell
you I'm sorry I lied about going home
and that I actually went to the zoo
instead. I just needed my space, baby. I
was just sick of having so much sex with
you. I mean I like it but I needed a
break. This beer is seriously like
ninety-degrees. Don't take this the
wrong way. I mean, you're pretty good at
doing-it. Clearly you have way more
experience than I do. I never even did
it with my own girlfriend.

Well, I couldn't legally 'cuz she's like
a kid or whatever. But the point is I
love doing it with you. The only weird
part is that sometimes you make noises.
Not bad noises, but like, you sometimes
sound like an animal from a farm. It's
okay, though. It's just distracting
sometimes. Forget about that. Jen. Baby.

26

Listen. Hey that's my roommate's. Put it
back. Derek Jeter signed it. Yes, he
did! It's real. Jen, listen. You know I
love yo—

    [SOUND OF GLASS BREAKING]

Fuck I have to piss.

    [SOUND OF BASEBALL BAT BEING
    URINATED ON]

    [END OF MESSAGE]

September 22

    Okay, I might go out tonight. Adam's sister (who's a senior) is having a party. I at first said I didn't want to go because I know we'll go to the bar afterward and I only have seven dollars and thirty-one cents in my account, but Ninja Nick and Adam talked me into it. I mean, if we do go to the bar, technically I can spend seven dollars and be fine.

I mean, I'd still have thirty-one cents in there, which wouldn't be good, but it also wouldn't be the end of the world. I won't spend too much. I can say "no."

You can't say "no!" : 50 cent Jello-shots!

SUNSETS

BAR AND GRILL

NO COVER!

LIVE MUSIC FRIDAYS!

JUKEBOX!

GOOD FRIENDS!

September 23

Alright here's what happened: We ended up going to the bars after Adam's sister's party. And I ended up spending six dollars. So I knew I had one dollar and thirty-one cents left in my account. Which is not that good, but I mean, it's above zero so I was like I'm cool, I'm cool.

Then Adam's sister—who is smoking hot— was like Donny buy me a Jello shot they're only fifty-cents. And I'm like oh man, I can't *not* buy her one, so I'm like okay, cool, I'll still have eighty-one cents in my account. Again, that's not a lot, but it's more than nothing. So I order her the Jello shot.

But then she's like, what, you're not gonna do one with me? And, like I said, this girl is smoking hot. So I give in and order myself one, too. Now I have thirty-one cents in my account, which blows, but I'm like whatever because I'm doing a Jello shot with Adam's hot sister who's a senior. Fine.

But *then* she goes oh get one for my roommate Theresa, too. And, of course, her roommate Theresa is drop-dead gorgeous. So I'm like, ok, they're only fifty-cents, so no matter what I'm not in *that* much trouble.

So I get three Jello shots and we do
them and I'm like awesome because I'm a
freshman and I just did Jello shots with two
hot senior girls.

So I am pretty sure I have negative
nineteen cents in my bank account. But I'm not
even worried because I can just go to the bank
tomorrow and deposit a quarter and be fine.
It's like, get over it, bank. You know? I had
a Jello shot, not a bottle of champagne.

September 24

Today is "Founder's Day" on campus, so
there weren't any classes. So we all (Ninja
Nick, New York Pete, Jersey—and get this—even
Steven and Steve) went to the gym. Jersey made
us all agree to try to go to the gym four
times a week together so we can stay in shape.
I think it's cool that we'll all have a bunch
of gym buddies or whatever to keep us
motivated and so we won't have to exercise
alone. But then I was thinking that Jersey
probably just wants to schedule things with me
so I'm not alone in his room eating his Cheez-
Its. Whatever.

Oh, and for some reason the bank wasn't
open today. That's fine. I'll just go tomorrow
and pay my big, scary, twenty-five cent fine
to the bank people. Cheap pricks.

September 25

I checked my bank balance today (at the bank's ATM, not the bookstore's which would charge me to do it) and check this out: somehow it's not negative. Not only is it not negative, but for some reason I have more money than I started out with. I don't know how, but a few days ago my balance was $7.31 and now it's $30.19. I almost went in to the bank and asked someone about it, but I thought no way I'll keep it! Bank error in my favor! This is like Monopoly haha!

```
----------------------------------------
      SAFEGUARD BANK -- KUL. BRANCH
----------------------------------------

     TERMINAL #        :DF4444221
     DATE              :09/25/2007

     CARD NUMBER       :XXXXXXXXXXXX4454

     DISPENSED AMOUNT  :00.00
     REQUESTED AMOUND  :00.00
     FROM ACCOUNT      checking

     TERMINAL FEE      :00.00
     ORIGINAL BALANCE  :(30.19)
     TOTAL AMOUNT      :00.00

     CURRENT BALANCE   :(30.19)
----------------------------------------
```

September 25

Science test tomorrow. Can't study in my room, though, because dickhead roommate James now blasts country music 24-7. I just want to be like yes, I know, you're from Texas. I get it. Enough already. (And by the way, I definitely think he's eating my Pop Tarts. I'm going to start keeping track.)

31

Anyway, Ugly Jen doesn't have a roommate so I'm headed to her room to study. I know what you're thinking, but no—study does not mean "study." It means *study*. I need to do good on this test.

September 26

I studied. That's it. Nothing else happened. I opened my physics book, read over chapters one through four, and left.
End of story. I swear nothing happened.

September 26

One time. We did it one time. I was stressed out! I had to! It was in between chapters two and three, and she put on some George Michael, and I felt bad because I was using her room to study and I thought I should repay her somehow. I didn't enjoy it. Are you kidding me? I can't stand that girl. She's hideous. Halfway through she started eating a Twix. That was new.

September 27

Took Ugly Jen out to dinner tonight. We went to Applebees. I figured why not, because the bank gave me free money anyway. It's not like it was a date. I was just hungry (*and of course she was*).

She tried kissing me goodnight. Yeah, right, Ugly Jen. You wish. I'm going to bed early. James has hillbilly country music station on TV so I might sleep on New York Pete's floor.

September 28

Ninja Nick ended up sleeping on New York Pete's floor last night, too. He's tiny but he kicks in his sleep. I had to curl up in a corner and use Jersey's dirty laundry as a pillow. I think I have bruises on my legs from Ninja Nick's sleeping ninja kicks.

This morning when I woke up Ninja Nick was standing over me, watching me. When I asked what he was doing he said, "Don't forget. You still owe me two favors." I said, "Ninja, I know. Stop being weird. What are the two favors?" But he just scampered away. So fucking bizarre.

Got physics test back. I did pretty good (B+) but I have way better news than that! I checked my bank account balance, just for fun, and I can't believe this but they must have screwed up again because I have even more money than before! I can understand the bank screwing up once, but twice? This is great! Oh, and check this out: someone from the bank called me today.

Probably calling to say oh we screwed up and gave you free money. Whatever! I'm not calling them back. They can't give me money and then take it back. I'm going out tonight. Big-time.

```
----------------------------------------
     SAFEGUARD BANK -- KUL. BRANCH
----------------------------------------

   TERMINAL #        :DF4444221
   DATE              :09/28/2007

   CARD NUMBER       :XXXXXXXXXXXX4454

   DISPENSED AMOUNT  :00.00
   REQUESTED AMOUNT  :00.00
   FROM ACCOUNT      checking

   TERMINAL FEE      :00.00
   ORIGINAL BALANCE  :(145.19)
   TOTAL AMOUNT      :00.00


   CURRENT BALANCE   :(145.19)

----------------------------------------
```

September 29

Wow. Last night was nuts. I think I spent a lot. Sixty, seventy bucks. Something like that. Ha. Who cares? It was free money. I gotta go. Jersey wants me to go to the gym with him.

```
        SUNSETS - BAR AND GRILL

            CUSTOMER BILL
   9/28/07

   BOTTLE BL (2)        4.00
   JELLOSHOT(37)       18.50
   SOUVENIR T-SHIRT(5) 50.00

   SUBTOTAL            72.50
   CARDNUMBER XXXXXXXXXXXX4454
   TIP
   TOTAL      72.50

   SIGNED  Donald Bl
```

```
        SUNSETS - BAR AND GRILL

            CUSTOMER BILL
```

September 30

Last night was so-so. Went out *again*, bought Adam's hot sister and her roommates drinks *again*, spent tons of free bank money *again*, shamefully slept with you-know-who *again*, etc. It's getting kind of boring. My life can be summed up in the following three-part sentence: Party all night, ravenously eat Jersey's Cheez-Its all day, and in between night and day have sex with a girl who is exceptionally not pretty.

Well, since I pretty much spent all that free bank money, I guess it's back to slim pickings for me. I should probably go deposit a quarter in my account tomorrow like I meant to do before I started getting all the free money. Maybe more than a quarter.

October 1

I can not believe it! The bank gave me even more money! This is unbelievable. I don't know what they did, but they keep doing it, and whatever "it" is is *absolutely fine* with me. It's like every time I go to the ATM I win a small lottery! Somehow, and I have no idea how, I had 150 bucks last week, spent it all at the bar…and made a couple hundred more without doing anything!

Right now my balance is…and I honestly can't believe this…three hundred thirty-five dollars and sixty-nine cents. If this keeps up, I won't have to finish college or get a job or anything! I'll just make my money the easy way. By finding it. In my bank account. For free. I am seriously considering dropping out of college. Let all these other suckers live in dorm rooms with Pop Tart-stealing roommates who listen to country-retard-redneck music with fake-autograph pissed-on bats. Who fucking needs it? I'm rich!

Now that I'm rich I should start dating super hot model chicks—not underage Keelie and ugly-ass Ugly Jen.

October 2

Broke up with both Keelie and Ugly Jen today. I think I ended things with both of them on a positive note. I don't think there's any hard feelings. I was just really honest with both of them.

DEAR JEN,

   The time has come for
us to address who we are as
a couple. Only, we're not a couple.
So I guess there's nothing left
to say.

                    Goodbye forever,

                    Donald Blake

P.S. I am dropping out of
   school because I am rich
   and you will never see me
   again. Goodbye forever.

P.P.S. Please do not call me
   any more (even though that
   should go without saying.)
            Goodbye forever.

37

FROM: DONNY MONEY BAGS@hotmail.com
TO: Keelie McNamara@StAnneHighSchool.edu

Keelie:

I have recently fallen on hard times. The Ghost Hunters did
not survive the exorcism of Ugly Jen's spirit. Apparently, she
was more than they bargained for. Consequently, my dorm is
now haunted by not only the spirit of Ugly Jen, but also the
spirits of the three recently deceased Ghost Hunters (T.J.,
Kent Brock, and Tommy Gemini). I have barricaded myself in
my room and my only contact with the outside world is
through my hillbilly roommate's computer (on which I am
typing right now). I should also point out that my hillbilly
roommate's computer is constantly playing really loud
country music (right now it's a song by Carrie Underwood)
and he has it on some security setting so I can't turn it off (or
even lower the volume). For that reason I find it impossible to
sleep and almost maddening to try to focus on typing this
email with the music so loud, and also that *I've dug my key
into the side of his pretty little supped up four-wheel-drive and
carved my name into his leather seeeeeeats...* Sorry. Like I
said, the music is up really loud. What I'm trying to say,
Keelie, is that we need to end things between us. I appreciate
all that you've done for me, but I am confident that I won't
ever see you again. In the case that we do meet again, I fear
that I will have already perished and have become an evil,
undead spirit/poltergeist. And I wouldn't want you to see me
like that, Keelie. Keep me in your heart always. Be safe at
prom next year. Goodbye forever.

Donny
P.S. Please don't call or email me back. It will only make
things harder. Goodbye forever.

October 3

Kyle, the weird and smelly kid, came into my room today (uninvited). He asked me if I knew what I was going to be for Halloween. At first I said are you fucking stupid Halloween is like eight weeks away you fucking smelly retard get the fuck out of my room. Then I felt bad and invited him back in.

I think he was just trying to make small-talk or something because he's had a hard time making friends at school. I believe this is due to his awful stench and his piss-poor social skills. I wanted to make him feel comfortable and so I decided to give in and talk about Halloween costumes. I said that I wanted to be something really scary for Halloween so could I borrow his face hahaha.

This particularly clever quip of mine did not elicit the reaction I was going for because Kyle immediately broke into tears. He collapsed on the floor, sobbing about how lonely he was at school and how nobody likes him and he doesn't know why.
I said Kyle get up off the floor and have a seat on my roommate's bed (if he has to get his stink on something let it at least be James' property, right?).

I told Kyle not to worry, lots of people have trouble adjusting to college life. For example, look at Ninja Nick. Kyle said does Ninja Nick even go to our school? I said good point, I'm not sure. Fine, I said, then how about me?

I've only been here for about a month and already I've cheated on my girlfriend from home countless times because of the pressures of this new independent lifestyle. I assured him that even when you think you've hit bottom that things will pick-up. And things did pick up for me, I said, because just look at this ATM receipt!

```
------------------------------------------
            KULHMAN BOOKSTORE ATM
------------------------------------------

        TERMINAL #        :D303421
        DATE              :10/02/07

        CARD NUMBER       :XXXXXXXXXXXX4454

        DISPENSED AMOUNT  :00.00
        REQUESTED AMOUNT  :00.00
        FROM ACCOUNT      checking

        TERMINAL FEE      :2.00
        ORIGINAL BALANCE  :(395.69)
        CURRENT BALANCE   :(397.69)

------------------------------------------
```

KU CAMPUS POLICE NOTES FOR THE WEEK OF 10/1 – 10/6

Wednesday, October 3 5:11pm

A freshman from Montgomery Hall was reported to have suddenly lost consciousness, and hit his head on a desk on the way down. A witness, also a freshman, says the subject fainted when he told him "what parentheses mean. You know, in banking terms." Another student, a female, noticed the student faint and immediately notified Campus Police using her mobile phone. Not wanting to wait for help to arrive, the female student hoisted the unconscious subject onto her wide, gorilla-like shoulders and trudged 1.4 miles across campus to Kulhman Health and Services. She claimed that she and the Freshman Fainter are involved in a tumultuous, up-and-down romance. When the subject regained consciousness he denied involvement in the romance. He was given handouts on fainting and other sleep-related medical ailments courtesy of the Health and Services staff. He was also given extensive literature on overdraft protection and ATM fraud courtesy of Safeguard Bank (KU Branch).

October 3

Kyle, my new friend, is enrolled in an introductory finance class. Thus, he has a command of banking knowledge just slightly ahead of my own. That slight difference in knowledge, however, allows him to understand the use of the parentheses. Apparently parentheses are not just used as valuable writing tools (they also can be used to show that your bank account balance is negative).

I (am (fucked)).

October 4

The bank, who has been calling me every day for a while now, called again today. I decided to answer. A helpful bank person informed me that for every day that my account is negative I am charged thirty dollars more (from the money that's not even there in the first place).

```
------------------------------------------
            KULHMAN BOOKSTORE ATM
------------------------------------------

    TERMINAL #          :D303421
    DATE               : 10/05/07

    CARD NUMBER        :XXXXXXXXXXXX4454

    DISPENSED AMOUNT   :00.00
    REQUESTED AMOUNT   :00.00
    FROM ACCOUNT        checking

    TERMINAL FEE       :2.00
    ORIGINAL BALANCE   :(491.69)
    CURRENT BALANCE    :(493.69)

------------------------------------------
```

October 5

I am up (down) to -$493.69. This situation is so grave that I cannot even find humor in the fact that the last two digits of this value are six and nine. At least they can't fine me on the weekend. I think.

October 6

By the way, Campus Police blew the whole "fainting" thing way out of proportion. Now I look like a sissy. *And* people think I'm in a "tumultuous up-and-down romance" with Ugly Jen (which couldn't be further from the truth).

10-6
1:15 PM
FROM: Keelie McNamara@StAnneHighSchool.edu
TO: DONNY MONEY BAGS@hotmail.com

Donny,

I have purchased a plane ticket and am on my way to see you.
We need to sort things out together. Will arrive tomorrow
afternoon.

Love you,
Keelie

P.S. I have thought ahead to bring holy water and other useful
ghost-fighting weapons.

October 7

Am not excited about Keelie coming to
visit. This could spell trouble. Maybe she's
bluffing. She wouldn't really come to visit me
would she? Here are the two main reasons I do
not want her to come:

1.   If Ugly Jen decides to be weird and stop
by, she'll see Keelie and flip out. Either
she'll scare Keelie to death with her horrid
ugliness or she'll start some big fight with
her (and I'm sure her ugly face gets even
uglier under the duress of a physical
confrontation).
2.   She is sixteen and everyone will think I'm
a pedophile.

October 8

Received frantic voicemail message from
Keelie. Her flight got held up in some
airport in Dayton, Ohio (where ever that is).
Whatever the reason for the delay is, I hope
it continues indefinitely because I don't want
Keelie to ever get here.

Also, I think I'm coming down with
something. I'm all stuffed-up and I can't stop
coughing.

October 9

    I don't know if it's the sudden cold weather or what, but I am *sick*. I didn't go to French class today. I did email the beautiful Madame Bierbaum-Cardeaux ahead of time, however. She is pretty or should I say *trés belle*. Hopefully she doesn't think I'm faking or something. The email was in French, so that must look good? I wrote "dear Madame, or whatever, how are you, I'm sick, I'm very sick, sorry, have a good day, Donny." That should be good enough. I did it really early this morning so I mean, I *think* that's what the email said. It's kinda hazy—I was sorta half asleep when I did it. Hope I didn't say anything stupid. Ughh, I feel awful. I just want to stay in bed all day.

10-9
8:03 AM
FROM: DONNY MONEY BAGS@hotmail.com
TO: bierbaumcardeaux@KU.edu

Madame,
Comme ca va? Je suis malade. Je suis trés malade. Desolé. Aussi, je pense que vous etes trés belle, et que vos lêvres sont forts et rouges. J'adore vos lêvres. Et vos hanches sont brillantes et circulaires. J'adore vos hanches, aussi.

Bon jour,
Donny

10-9
11:21 AM
FROM: bierbaumcardeaux@KU.edu
TO: DONNY MONEY BAGS@hotmail.com

Donny,
I will type this email in English. While I do appreciate that
you wrote me in French, I want to make this message as clear
(and un-confusing) as possible.

I received your email from this morning. It was very concise
and to-the-point at the start ("How are you, I'm sick, I'm very
sick, sorry"). That part was fine. I understand—students live
in dorms, germs get passed around, and people get sick. As
you know, my attendance policy is very generous and you can
make up the work.

The part of your message I was concerned about was the
second paragraph. I'll translate your words for you:

> *"Also, I think that you are very pretty, and that your lips
> are strong and red. I love your lips. Your hips are shiny
> and round. I love your hips, also.*
>
> *Good day,*
> *Donny."*

I can only assume that your remedial knowledge of the French
language has tripped you up in some way and that you were
trying to say something else. I would find it shocking if you
really were trying to flirt with your French professor in an
email. Or perhaps your sickness is the cause of this bizarre
behavior. I mean, you did describe my "hips" as "shiny," and
my "lips" as "strong." Wouldn't it be the other way around?
In any case, I will see you next class. Please look over your
verb conjugation chart as there is an upcoming quiz.

Madame

October 9

Great. Now Madame Bierbaum-Cardeaux thinks I'm in love with her. Maybe I can send her flowers or something so she doesn't think I'm so strange. Actually, she'd probably take that the wrong way, too. Plus, I'm not sure what type of flowers I could afford for negative five hundred dollars.

Speaking of negative money, I talked to someone else from the bank today. I asked them if they could stop fining me while I try to figure this whole mess out. They said ok and that my account will remain frozen at -553.69.

Keelie is still in Dayton, Ohio. I think she has been sleeping in the waiting areas of the airport, so I'm sure she'll be nice and cranky when she shows up. With my luck she'll probably be on her period, too, which will only add to her crankiness. (Is she even old enough to get a period? I honestly don't know.)

Still sick.

October 10

    Still sick. Missed classes again today. Made an appointment to see a doctor tomorrow at Health Services. I'm sure they'll be surprised to see me walk in on my own, and not sleepingly carried in by gross (and strong) Ugly Jen. I think Keelie will finally be able to fly here tomorrow. Ugh.

    I don't think Jersey likes that I'm sick. He's at the gym right now, and he gave me a dirty look when I said I was too sick to go with him today. Whatever, I couldn't even eat Cheez-Its right now. I'm too sick.

    Maybe I should grab some for when I get better, though. Maybe just a bag.

October 11

    Figured out what I'm going to do about Keelie: I'm going to tell everyone that she's my little sister. That way it won't look so weird that a high school girl is coming to visit me. Speaking of high school—is she just missing like an entire week of classes, or what?

    And I'll just hope that stupid Ugly Jen doesn't show up out of nowhere and bring her dead-body-looking face with her and make a big, ugly scene.

OUTBOX
To: NEW YORK PETE, JERSEY, ADAM
Sep 6, 1:14AM

HEY MY LITTLE SISTER IS COMING TO VISIT TODAY BUT I
HAVE A DOCTOR APPT. WHEN SHE SHOWS UP COULD
YOU KEEP HER BUSY? THX

October 11

    Everything seems to be working perfectly. Everyone thinks Keelie is my sister and somehow even *she* hasn't caught on to it. I am so smooth.

    Doctor gave me some antibiotic pills. They taste bad. Have been washing them down with Cheez-Its.

October 12

Last night Keelie and I had a big talk about our relationship. And ghosts. And my enormously negative bank account. She sprinkled holy water on my doorframe, which was nice of her, and then offered to pay off my negative balance.

I told her no, and that I couldn't accept money from her. She then explained that technically the money would be coming from her father. I said then in that case, yes, I *could* accept the money. Paying off this negative balance means a tremendous weight off my shoulders, and so it's good news.

However, that means that I can't break things off with Keelie, which is bad news. You can't take $500 from a girl's father and then dump her!

Also: I forgot all about my verb conjugations quiz in French class… but I somehow aced it!

October 13

Barbershop 2: Back in Business was playing on campus, so Keelie and I went to see it. Laughing so hard made her tired, so I wasn't surprised that she wanted to make it an early night. We were in bed by 11. I am missing approximately two Pop Tarts.

51

October 14

Keelie left today. It was sorta sad to see her go. Mainly because I didn't know how she wanted to handle the money issue. (Like am I supposed to wait for a check in the mail, or...?)

I feel bad because while Keelie was here I sorta just spent time with her and didn't really hang out with anyone else. But, the thing is, I haven't really even *seen* anyone else around lately. It's almost like people are avoiding me or something (haha, yeah right).

I'll admit it, it was nice to have Keelie around for a few days. It'll be weird sleeping alone tonight. It was so nice to have someone in bed next to me, someone from home. It made being at this new place, college, a little less scary. At first, I was considering having Keelie sleep in a girl's dorm room or something, to make it look more like she was actually my sister. But what girls do I even know who live in dorms (aside from Ugly Jen)?

Plus, who would even notice if she slept in my room with me? I'm sure real siblings share bedrooms all the time.

October 14

Someone just slid a note under my door. At first I thought it was another RA note from Kenny. But it's not on Kulhman letterhead. And for some reason it's not signed? I think maybe it's from Jeff, because there's so much about God in it. It says something about the "dangers of laying with your own kin" and how it's sinful to eat the fruit of my own tree or some stupid shit like that. I don't even know what that means. It's hard to understand— he probably thinks I'm Jewish or something and is trying to convert me. Whatever. I'm off to bed.

October 15

After class today I stopped into Jersey's room to grab another bag of Cheez-Its. You won't believe what I found on his desk: a note to me from Keelie!
She must have written me before she left and somehow one of my idiot hallmates found it. Anyway, I think the note explains why everyone's been giving me the cold shoulder. And Jeff's note from the other day makes a lot more sense now.

Donny,

By the time you read this I will have already left and gone back to my boring high school life. I wish more than anything that I could stay here with you. I have had so much fun with you and have seen a side of you that I haven't seen before.

It felt so good to sleep next to you in your tiny dorm-room bunk bed. With your arm around me, I knew I was just so safe. Safe from danger, safe from the stresses of high school, and most of all, <u>safe from ghosts.</u>

What I really want to tell you is that I think I am ready to take our relationship to the next level. What I mean is that I want to show you just how much I really love you. In a physical way. <u>I'm ready to have intercourse with you, Donny.</u> That's the real reason I helped you pay-off your negative bank account balance: because I wanted you to know that I care about you enough to give my body to you completely. I want to take things further than just "first base" for once. I've known you my whole life, and I think we owe it to each other to do this.

And I don't care if I'm only sixteen. It's my body and I can do whatever I want with it, <u>no matter what our parents' say.</u>

Can't wait to see you again,

Keelie

October 15

Apparently everyone thinks I have a romantic (and soon-to-be sexual) relationship with my little sister. I have been weighing the implications of Keelie's visit very carefully:

PRO: No more negative bank balance. Hurray!

CON: I have to keep dating Keelie because her dad gave me money.

PRO: Keelie wants to take the "next step" with me.

CON: My friends think my little sister wants to take the "next step" with me.

PRO: I got to see Barbershop 2: Back in Business, starring Ice Cube and Cedric the Entertainer.

CON: My friends think my little sister wants to take the "next step" with me.

PRO: Ugly Jen didn't show up once while Keelie was here.

And finally...

CON: My friends think my little sister wants to take the "next step" with me.

October 16

We had another French quiz today (why so many?)! And I definitely didn't study for it, so I'm not looking forward to getting it back. I need to get like a planner or something, to write down assignments and homework reminders. (*I wonder if I could find a planner that has a daily horoscope thing in it?)

Oh, and yeah, everyone still thinks I'm dating my little sister.

October 17

I've been thinking more about this whole "everyone thinks I'm dating my little sister" thing, and I found one more pro...

PRO: If Ugly Jen thinks I'm dating my little sister, that could repulse her so much that she might want nothing to do with me ever again. This is the best pro, really, because nothing would be better than getting Ugly Jen out of my life forever. Speaking of Ugly Jen, where has she been? I haven't heard from her in a while. I mean, like I care. I hope she transferred!

October 18

I got a 95 on that French quiz from the Tuesday. I must be so good (*bon*) at French (*le français*) that I don't have to study (*etudier*). Great: that's one less thing I have to worry about.

Also, it seems that weird, smelly Kyle is the only hallmate who isn't currently shunning me for my (alleged) incestuous relationship with my (fake) little sister. Probably because when you're as weird and as smelly as Kyle is, you have to take what you can get.

Kyle and I went to the gym together, without the rest of the guys. This was helpful in two ways. First, it gave me a workout partner. Second, I didn't have to raid Jersey's closet alone for a post-workout Cheez-Its feast. Kyle likes Cheez-Its, too.

October 19

Seriously—where is Ugly Jen?

October 20

    Didn't go out last night. I mean, I would
have, but no one invited me. I guess it's not
"cool" or whatever to hang out with someone who
you think is having sex with his sister.
Whatever. Hypocrites.

    Anyway, last night Adam and his girlfriend
came back around two and saw me in the hallway.
I think because Adam was drunk he decided to
talk to me. He said something like, "It really
doesn't affect me if you and your sister bang.
She's hot; I'd do it." I tried explaining that
Keelie isn't my sister but then his girlfriend
was like, "Donny, we don't care.
Adam and I are very open about our own
sexuality and we would never judge you and your
sister's relationship."

    Then they started to have sex in the
hallway so I went into my room and watched TV
for a while. As I was flipping through the
channels, *Charm School* came on VH-1 and I
thought of texting Ugly Jen. There's this ugly,
loud girl on the show who looks sorta like her.

October 21

    I wonder what Ugly Jen is going to be for
Halloween. I wonder if *Charm School* is on
tonight.

October 22

I couldn't sleep last night. I don't know what it was. It's not that I miss her, or even like her, but, seriously—where the fuck is Ugly-fucking-Jen? What's her fucking problem?!

Who does she think she is that she can just drop off the fucking face of the earth? What the fuck is this, a cartoon? I'm not going to school today.

October 22

I *did* go to school today. I was just late for a class, that's all. Whatever. Ugly Jen isn't even worth it. I can have any girl I want. On the way back to the dorm today I was looking around campus, and I thought to myself, "I can make-out with any girl here."

And it's true. I could. <u>Any girl at this school</u>. And I thought about everything I've done so far at college—making new friends, buying Adam's sister Jello shots at the bar, getting *into* a bar in the first place, breaking a bathroom window, doing awesome in French class, lifting weights all the time...I mean, the list goes on and on. I am starting to realize just how awesome I really am.

Also, a check came in the mail today from Keelie's father.

October 23

Madame Bierbaum-Cardeaux was really, really nice to me today. I stuck around after class to ask her about some things I'm having trouble with (using the past tense of verbs, etc) and she helped me a lot. She had me come back to her office with her to talk about the lesson. That was nice. She had me practice conjugating some sentences at her desk. She even helped me pronounce some words better by putting her finger on my lips and guiding my mouth to make the right shapes when I talked. That should help my French accent, especially with words that start with **o, e** and **u** (those are the ones that trip me up!). It sorta tickled to have her finger tracing the outline of my lips. And sometimes she slipped and her finger sorta touched like inside my lips or whatever but it was cool. It's for the best—I gotta learn this stuff.

I've been really bummed out lately about stupid Ugly Jen, but Madame Bierbaum-Cardeaux really put me in a good mood!

October 24

In between classes today Adam and I talked about Halloween costumes. His sister is having a costume party this Saturday so we want to do this right. We narrowed it down to three or four pretty good ideas. I'm not going to list them here, though, in case someone reads this and steals them. (I wonder what James is going as for Halloween. Maybe The Pop Tart Burglar? That way he wouldn't need a costume. Get it?)

Anyway, I stopped by Madame Bierbaum-Cardeaux's office to get a little bit more help with French. Thank god she had time, because we have a test tomorrow and I really want an A. Madame has a nice office. She also smelled pretty good today. I mean, she always smells good, but something about her perfume today was extra…I dunno.

She gave me her cell number, just in case I had any last minute questions before our test tomorrow. That was pretty nice of her. I mean, I doubt I would call, but that was cool. By giving me her number, she is sorta saying, hey Donny, I trust you to not prank me. Madame has a way of making me feel mature. Like a man!

Still no word from Ugly Jen. What-the-fuck-ever, Uggo Jenno. I guess I'll be sweet-talking other smoking hot chicks in French and not you. Jerk.

October 25

I think the whole "everyone thinks I'm dating my sister" thing has blown over because Ninja Nick and Adam invited me to go out with them tonight. Either they know I was lying and that Keelie isn't really my sister, or they still think she is my sister and are okay with the fact that I'm dating her. Either way is fine with me!

French exam was piece of cake. (Oh, I could go for some cake right now!)

October 26

Halloween Party tonight! I really pushed for the Hitler and Eva Braun costume, but we couldn't find anything to wear for that. So we decided to do Groom and Runaway Bride. After checking several thrift stores we found an old wedding dress. Of course *I* had to be the bride. Here's the way I see it: Adam wants to be the groom? Fine. At least I'm not the one getting ditched on my wedding day. Sucker.

October 27

Our costume was a big hit at Adam's
sister's party. As it turns out, Jeff dressed
up as a priest (big surprise, I know) so we
kept having him "marry" us in front of people.
But when he would say, "You may now kiss the
bride" I would try to kiss a nearby girl
instead of Adam. And then I would run. Because
I was the Runaway Bride. I wouldn't run that
far, though (it's hard to run in a wedding
dress!). Anyway the party was really fun.

I think we're having a party in our
hallway tonight. I'm sorta beat from the whole
Halloween thing, though—I didn't get to bed
until like 5am. And I kept having to wake up
and pee which was hard because I still had the
wedding dress on and that made peeing very
difficult.

Oh, by the way—good thing we didn't do
the whole Hitler and Eva Braun thing because
tons of people did that. What an oddly popular
costume?

October 28

Time to relax. I am not going to do
anything today. I feel like a train crashed
into me or something. I am just exhausted.

October 28

As exhausted as I am, I sorta can't wait for French class. So I think I'll go over some vocab or something before bed.

10-28
9:58 PM
FROM: bierbaumcardeaux@KU.edu
TO: DONNY MONEY BAGS@hotmail.com

Chèr Donny,

How are you? I know it's the weekend and we don't have to meet for class until Tuesday but I just wanted to check in and say Hi. I'm sure you had a busy weekend filled with parties and pretty girls (by the way do you have a girlfriend?). So you probably don't want to hear from an old lady like me (well I'm not that old!). I just wanted to let you know that I gave you my number for a reason. If you ever have any questions about class, or anything else, anything else at all, please call me. I think of you as a very special student that I can relate to. I have never been so fond of a student or trusted a student so much to give him my private number. So I encourage you to take advantage of that. I know we may have gotten off on the incorrect foot when you sent that adorable email to me and I shouldn't have been so hard on you. It is comforting to know that you think my "hips are shiny and round." Please enjoy what's left of your Sunday evening.

Au revoir,
Madame

10-28
10:03 PM
FROM: bierbaumcardeaux@KU.edu
TO: DONNY MONEY BAGS@hotmail.com

Chèr Donny,

I'm sorry to write you again so soon but I wanted to ask your advice
on a matter. Earlier this morning I went to the coffee shop with my
Monsieur, Phillipe (who you should know is a complete buffoon).
We entered the café (he did not hold the door for me, by the way)
and placed our orders. He immediately started sweet-talking the
cashier. He denies this and insists it was just "making conversations"
and "innocent" but I can tell otherwise. I know when he is doing
flirting with the woman. Which is why I wanted to bring this up to
you, Donny. What do you think I should do? Is this a concern that I
should be having that my man is not full of love for me anymore? I
apologize if my English at this current point is not flawless—I am
emotionally distressed and feel that you are someone I can trust.
Since you are a man.

I await your response.

Au revoir,

Madame

10-28
10:11 PM
FROM: bierbaumcardeaux@KU.edu
TO: DONNY MONEY BAGS@hotmail.com

Cher Donny,

I am sorry to write a third time to you this evening, but I just have
nothing else to do since I am sleeping alone tonight. Yes, I decided
to stay at my own place and not at Phillipe's. Phillipe the Buffoon, I
should call him. He is a big buffoon who has not respect for me but
only for himself. I deserve someone who respects me for my mind,
and not just for the sensual pleasures I can provide.

Anyway, I hope you do not think me a crazy woman because I have
emailed you so much tonight. It's just lonely in this apartment
without anyone else. Lonely and dark. I'm actually a bit worried
about that. Because of how bad the crime is in this country. I have no
one here to protect me, you know. Not like in my office at the
University, such as when you visit for help. When you are there,
Donny, in my office with me, when we are studying, I feel that it is a
very safe place. Because of you are there with me. Something about
you makes me feel safe.

Well, I will stop bothering you for the night I suppose. I should
probably try to sleep—although my bed is so large that I might get
lost in it, just me in this big bed built for two. There is a bright side, I
suppose, because since I am alone I can sleep naked for all anyone
cares. Mon dieu, don't think me a crazy woman, Donny!

I will see you Tuesday.

Bon soir,
Madame

October 29

    I feel like freshman year is moving way
too fast for me.

66

October 30

Tons of stuff happened today! Firstly, Ninja Nick got all his photos from the Halloween party developed. (I know, I know, if he's so Asian then why doesn't he just get a really high-tech digital camera?) Anyway, the pictures are photographic evidence that our costume idea of Runaway Bride and Groom was super fucking sweet.

Also, weirdsmelly Kyle (I have combined the words "weird" and "smelly" into one word, *weirdsmelly*, for convenience) stopped by my room today and asked me about laundry. *Laundry*. Are you fucking kidding me? Laundry? What a fucking tool. Anyway he wanted to know really dumb things like how much detergent you're supposed to use, how often you should clean your clothes, if you're supposed to dry them before you fold them, just really stupid common sense things.

At first I thought he was kidding but quickly realized that he really didn't understand the concept of doing laundry. So then I felt fucking awesome because this poor weirdsmelly kid needed help with his life and he came *to me*. I said listen, Kyle, laundry isn't a hard thing to get good at.

Basically you take clothes that have been worn and put them in the washing machine, put in a very arbitrary amount of detergent and turn the washer on. You take the clothes out when they're done, and you put 'em in the dryer. Piece of cake. But then Kyle was like, Donny, I do all that stuff and my clothes all still smell. And I was like, yeah, you do smell. That's one thing I've noticed about you since I moved in here, is that you are smelly. Then I was like, this is good for him to hear, he needs to know, so I said the second thing I've noticed about you is that you are weird. And when I refer to you either in my journal or to other people I have to specify that I'm talking about "Kyle, the weird and smelly kid."

He started to turn real red and get real sweaty because I think he was embarrassed. I said Kyle, listen, you need to hear this. And you're getting all sweaty and, thus, more smelly. You are only proving the hurtful things that I'm saying about you. And I think he was taking this all really well so I decided to let him in on my recent word-invention, *weirdsmelly*. I think at this point he was feeling so many emotions that he wasn't able to talk. He was, however, still able to stink. Badly. Echh. Oh, well.

I think I'm going to take Kyle on as a personal project of mine. You know, like that movie with Freddie Prinze Jr. where he takes the ugly girl and makes her hot. I'm gonnna take weirdsmelly Kyle and make him normal or something. Only I won't date him. You know what I mean.

(Oh, I forgot to mention that after French class today Madame Bierbaum-Cardeaux asked if I wanted to get together for a drink later tonight.)

October 31

Trick or Treat! So, as it turns out I am what you call a "good kisser" in French. Don't freak out, it's not what you think, there was nothing romantic, or sexual (or predatory) going on. Madame and I went out last night just to talk. And to "kick it." And even though we're just friends she explained that it's a European custom to kiss goodnight, no matter what. Everyone over there does it, she says. I said that I've seen movies where Europeans smooch each other on the cheek, but she said that the *real* way to do it is to use your tongues. Maybe that's why America is so screwed up, I told her, because there's not as much deep-tongue kissing between professors and students.

69

Still, though, I think I should keep all this pretty hush-hush because if what's-her-face (Keelie) found out, she wouldn't approve. Keelie doesn't really know much about foreign customs. I don't think she'd understand that in France it's perfectly normal for a 44-year old teacher to make-out with her 19-year old student. Not to be a jerk, but Keelie is pretty closed-minded.

November 1

Boring day, not much to report except that I think James went on vacation or something? When I woke up this morning I noticed that most of his clothes were gone and so were his bed sheets. And that my Missing Pop Tart Count hasn't changed. I don't know what his deal is because it's definitely not Spring Break yet. It's not even Thanksgiving break yet. Jeez, it's *not even Friday yet*. Maybe there was some big country music festival that he had to get to just to remind himself how much of a fucking redneck-retard-hill-fucking-billy he is.

November 2

I applied for an on-campus job today. You know, just to have some spending money. In case what's her face's (Keelie's) dad's money runs out.

James is definitely gone, so I decided to pee all over his mattress. It was kinda my personal way of saying, "Since you aren't here I'm going to pee on your bed." Very satisfying.

November 2

Bad idea peeing on James' mattress. Whole room stinks. (Like pee.) Maybe Kyle wants to clean it for me. It could be good way to test his friendship.

Kuhlman University
APPLICATION FOR EMPLOYMENT
BIOLOGY LAB ASSISTANT

Name: **DONALD BLAKE**

Year in school: **FRESH**

Hours available to work during the school week:
Not that much I just want extra drinking
money for weekends. Just kidding I will
use any and all money earned to only
spend on responsible things that matter.
(Like soap and Band Aids.)

Are you a Biology Major or a Pre-Med student?
No. I wanted to do Art History or
Accounting but unfortunately Kulhman does
not offer such programs.

What characteristics about yourself qualify you to be a
Biology Lab Assistant?
I have always had a great rapport with
others and have clean eating habits and
immensely respect the entire world of
biology. This includes plants and insects
as well as people and the inventions that
people have come up with through all of
the civilizations of earth's mankind.

***And if I may say, I have been known as
a "very handsome" person as well as a
"great person to talk to about personal
stuff." Please contact any or all of my
references to verify this fact.

References:
Madame Bierbaum-Cardeaux, French
Professor, ext. 5387

72

November 4

   Surprise, surprise—guess who left me
a voicemail last night? Yep. Ugly Jen.
Can you believe it? She said I needed to
call her back or come see her "as soon as
possible." Ha. Stupid Ugly Jen doesn't
know there's an easier way to say that
("ASAP").

November 5

   It's Monday and still no sign of
James. I've been looking around and it
seems that all of his stuff is gone.
Everything. Weird. Ugly Jen called and
left another ugly message on my phone.
Ha. She must really "want it."

INBOX
From: Hot French Prof
Nov 6, 3:14AM

DID YOU LIST ME AS A REFERNCE FOR SOMETHING? THE
BIO LAB PHONED ME

OUTBOX
To: Hot French Prof
Nov 6, 3:16AM

OUI, MADAME

November 7

I got hired at the biology lab! The pay is seven an hour and all I have to do is clean stuff up and file reports for the professors. Easy! I start on Thursday.

In other news, I got like five more messages from Ugly Jen. And Ninja Nick said that she stopped by my room while I was in class. Jeez! I know earlier I wrote that she must really "want it" but I mean she must really want *it*! From *me*! Trust me, I made it perfectly clear to Ugly Jen from **day one** that I was a "playa." I was like, listen, Ugly Jen, I ain't your man. I can't be tied down. She knew I was only in it for the "action." Wow, that "action" must have made quite an impact on poor Ugly Jen. She must have fallen in love with me. Or fallen in love with my sex techniques!

Transcript of voice message left on mobile phone of DONALD BLAKE on Wednesday November 7 at 6:18 PM:

Donny. I don't know why you're ignoring my messages. It's Jennifer. I need you to call me back. I know you're probably mad at me for sorta dropping out of your life. I know I probably led you on when I said that I'd be with you forever. I know that after we'd have sex, I mean, if you could call it that…most of the time you wouldn't actually be able to, um, perform, but I mean, it wasn't a big deal. I mean, I don't know if you were nervous or if I intimidated you or what? But anyway, after we'd do *whatever you wanna call what we did*, I remember how I'd hold you in my arms like a scrawny little baby and you'd start crying and sucking your thumb. And I know that you thought I wanted to care for you, and mother you, and love you forever. By the way, what was with that? The thumb thing, I mean. I thought only like toddlers sucked their thumbs.

Anyway. I know you're probably all broken-up inside and I feel awful.

75

But I do need to talk to you. And I
don't mean to lead you on again— I'm
actually kinda dating someone else.
Well, not dating, but I dunno. We're
talking. I'm sure you understand.
Anyway, just to reiterate: I don't want
you back or anything like that. I just
have something to tell you, and I'd
rather not do it over a voicemail.
Please call me back. Thank you. Bye. By
the way, I stopped by your room earlier.
Did your roommate move out or something?

[END OF MESSAGE]

November 8

    Had my first day of work in the biology
lab. It was just as easy as I thought it'd be.
And boring. Oh my god so fucking boring. My
boss is very odd. "Dr. Tolar." Something fishy
about him. The only cool part of the lab was
when I got to help put away the fetal pigs.
Fetal pigs are these tiny little baby pigs
that they dissect. They keep them in this big
cooler. Also, after French class today Madame
talked to me and she seemed sorta irked (is
that a real word? I heard one of the bio
professors say that today and I didn't know if
it was a real word or not but I thought I'd
try using it somewhere safe, like in my
journal. "Doesn't it irk you when you're late
for class?" "I'm irked because my feet are so
sore." "Quit irking me around." "Stop being
such a fucking irk." "Irk you, asshole.") that
I listed her as a reference for the biology
lab job. I guess she wants to keep our
friendship or whatever more private, and wants
to make sure as far as the University is
concerned all we are is teacher and student
and nothing more. And she's worried that my
job application is physical evidence of an
elicit relationship or some shit, blah blah
blah. I guess French people are just worry
warts. And worry warts irk me.

November 9

Went to gym with everyone today. I even managed to get Kyle (weirdsmelly) to come with us. It was fun to hang out with the guys and just get down and lift some weights. Felt very manly. Like a caveman (a tough caveman Hunter, not a little pussy caveman Gatherer).

So at one point we were all talking about girls and all the girls we've hooked-up with so far this semester. Of course I had to talk about Ugly Jen. And of course I had to talk about Keelie. And of course I had to point out, again, that Keelie is not really my sister. A few guys are still very skeptical and insist that I am an incestuous pervert (though they accept me nonetheless).

When I was done sharing my hook-up stories everyone seemed sorta disappointed. Kinda like I didn't have enough juicy stuff to tell. And I didn't wanna look like a little bitch(or gay!) so I was like, "I made-out with one of my teachers." Then I thought *that still doesn't prove I'm not gay,* so I pointed out that the teacher was a female. Then they were like, "Which teacher?" and I was like, "My French teacher" and they were like "No fucking way, Donny, we don't believe you" and I was like "I swear to God I've made-out with her tons of times.

She's French, it's what they do" and they were like "Whatever you fucking gay liar" and I was like "I'm not gay already. And who would care if I was? I'm pretty sure Jersey's gay and no one gives him any shit" and Jersey was like "Yeah I'm gay so what? Fuck you" and I was like "See?" and they were like "Fine, but you still didn't make-out with your female French teacher" and I was like "Yes I fucking did and I can do it any fucking time I want!" and they were like "Prove it!" and I was like "Fine!"

And then I thought to myself: *Man, am I irked.*

November 10

Adam's sister had another party last night. I invited Madame Bierbaum-Cardeaux to come with us, but she declined the offer. (She did suggest that maybe we get together afterward for a late-night cocktail, but I told her that I'd probably be drunk and that would be a bad idea because knowing me I'd make a hateful French slur or something.) Party was fun. Kyle (weirdsmelly) came with us. Despite his distinctive qualities of weirdsmelly, he is starting to fit in with our group of friends.

Jersey was at first upset with me for "outing" him at the gym, but then expressed his gratitude to me and said he felt "free" to be himself. Whatever the fuck that means.

Saw ants in my room. Followed their stupid little ant trail and discovered a long-lost open bag of Cheez-Its underneath M.I.A. James' bed. Made ants share with me.

Kuhlman University

2900 Salvage Parkway
Tomaschevske, OH 46121

RE: Missing Roommate

Donald:

You may have noticed that you haven't seen your roommate, James
Kovach, in a few days. You may have also noticed that all of his
stuff is gone. You're probably thinking to yourself, "Man. My
roommate is gone." You're thinking correctly.

James decided to drop his classes for the semester and move back
home with his family. Another student may or may not be assigned
to your room, depending on how things pan out for the rest of the
semester. For now, feel free to enjoy the life of having your own
room (within reason).

I understand that there can be some loneliness in a situation like this.
You may feel guilty, or that you are somehow responsible for James
dropping out of college. While I would like to assure you that it's not
your fault, I cannot (legally or morally) do that. I assume his
situation has something to do with money or family, but for all I
know you could quite possibly be the reason he left. In any case, if
you need to talk to someone about this, we have a very qualified staff
at Kulhman Health Services that would welcome your call (or visit).

Also, please take care of the ant problem in your room. The colony
has been expanding its operation and we have found tiny little ant
explorers in many different hallways. I know that Kulhman
University is known as the "famed glove-box of the Midwest"
because of its rich and tremendous appreciation of immigration and
culture-melding, but this does not apply to insects. (Maybe your
roommate moved out because you are gross and attract ants?)

Thank you,
Kenny
ex. 4499

INBOX
From: Hot French Prof
Nov 11, 9:56 PM

SUP? U AWAKE? TXT ME BCK

INBOX
From: Hot French Prof
Nov 11, 10:17 PM

WATCHING THAT CHARM SCHOOL SHOW YOU TOLD ME
ABOUT- DONT SEE THE APPEAL. TXT OR CALL ME

November 11

Feeling stressed out. Three tests this week. Plus I have to work in the biology lab every night this week. Dr. Tolar is kind of a demanding boss (I still think there's something fishy about him). It's fine. I need the money. I just didn't know I'd be working so much.

I don't know what Kenny's fucking deal is with his racism against ants. They aren't bothering anybody. In fact, they're helping me find snacks. Any time I've been hungry lately I just follow one of their trails and if it doesn't lead back to their busy lair it leads to a tasty treat. They're completely friendly. Fucking Kenny. He's anti-ant. He's like the Hitler for ants. He's Antler. I'm not killing any of them. I refuse! Must study more.

November 11

Dozed off while studying. Awakened by an ant crawling across my nose. The ant colony and I seem to have developed a mutual respect for each other and we can communicate on some very remedial levels. I think he wanted to let me know that someone was knocking on my door. I thanked him and answered my door. It was Ninja Nick. He had a black eye and was sorta crying. He reminded me that I owed him two favors and wanted to know if he could cash one of them in. I said absolutely. I told Ninja Nick to calm down and had the ants bring him some Cheez-Its. Will write more later.

November 11

It seems that Ugly Jen's new boyfriend or whatever decided to give Ninja Nick a black-eye. (Too bad Ninja Nick isn't a real ninja otherwise he would have iced that dude.) So he wants me to get this guy back somehow. This is one of the favors I owe him. I'm not yet sure what I'm going to do to get this guy back but it will be good, trust me. Anyway, I gotta get to the biology lab. I think a new shipment of fetal pigs came in today. I swear, that place goes through so many fetal pigs I don't know how they keep track of them.

November 11

    They don't keep track of them.

November 11

    I have a plan.

November 12

    I have stolen one fetal pig from the biology lab. That's like one out of literally hundreds. Dr. Tolar will not notice. Well, I mean, when I set the thing on fire in front of Ugly Jen's new boyfriend's house tonight he might notice. Or maybe I'll do it tomorrow night. It depends 'cuz I have to study a lot this week.

    Ants are doing well. From what I can tell, and I know this might not be exact, this is our mutual human/ant agreement:

1. I will allow the ants to colonize my room and the adjacent inner-walls, ceiling, etc.

2. Of any tasty foods they discover in their explorations, approximately one-third of their booty will be given to me as tribute.

3. They agree to not bite me or crawl in my sheets.

4. I agree to not kill/ethnically cleanse the ant colony.

    It's like I lost one asshole roommate and gained forty-thousand awesome ones!

Kuhlman University

2900 Salvage Parkway
Tomaschevske, OH 46121

RE: Ants

Donald:

The ant infestation has gotten out of control. I have received complaints from several students (both in your hallway and in the hallways above and below yours) as well as from the cleaning crew. The ants' voyages to discover and take food all seem to lead back to your room. In one way or another, it is clear that you are responsible for this problem.

As a representative and active member of the Kuhlman University Resident Staff I must ask you one more time to take care of the ant problem. Ants are filthy creatures who walk beneath our feet. They do not deserve to live in a dormitory as nice as this one. In fact, they don't belong on *any* college campus. They belong in the dirt, crawling on their disgusting bellies like the vermin they are. They are not like us, Donny. They aren't human. They are animals. Vile, repulsive, six-legged beasts. You have until Friday to get rid of "them."

One more thing: we will be having a Thanksgiving Week Potluck Feast in the Common Room this Saturday. Pilgrim/Native American attire is strongly encouraged (though technically not required). Hope to see you there, Donny!

Thank you,
Kenny
ext. 4499

November 13

Have stolen a second fetal pig. Will set fire to it outside Kenny's room. But not tonight. Too much studying to do. (Remember to explain the dangers of fire to the ants. Also remember to go shopping for Pilgrim outfit for Thanksgiving Week Potluck Feast. That sounds pretty fun! And finally, remember to tell Jersey that I've been storing a pair of fetal pigs in his mini-fridge.)

November 14

Ugly Jen keeps calling. Yeah, right, Ugly Jen. Like I'm gonna have sex with you after your new boyfriend punched my ninja in the face. Get real. I'm so fucking irked right now. Stupid Ugly Jen. I'll take her back when pigs fly. **Or when they burn.** Must study more.

November 15

Jersey (now gay) showed me this new calf
exercise today. We both feel that my calves
could use a lot of work. I want jacked fucking
calves. I do not feel this makes me gay.

Madame Bierbaum-Cardeaux expressed
interest in having a dinner/study date
sometime this weekend for the upcoming final.
I thought this might be a good idea (even
though the final is like five weeks away?) so
we settled on Sunday night.

Guess what! I saw Ugly Jen on campus
today. She didn't see me, though, thank god.
She was walking out of the Health and Services
building. Man did she put on some pounds.
Gross.

Adam's sister is letting us use her
house tonight to have a freshman party. But
instead we're just going to have a Box of Wine
Race for our friends. We're having teams of
two and you have to race to finish an entire
box of wine.

Teams are as follows (listed in order of how I
predict they will finish:

1. Jersey and New York Pete
2. Fargo and Bryan
3. Me and Ninja Nick
4. Adam and his Girlfriend
5. Jeff and God (he's always bragging about how close of friends they are, now it's time to prove it)
6. Kyle Weirdsmelly and James (Kyle hasn't noticed that James moved out so we're just going to pretend that he's really late and act surprised when he never shows up)
7. Steven and Steve

I have a History test tomorrow so I have to hurry up and finish studying before Wine Time. Or maybe I can just study after the race?

Ants are doing very well. The Queen must be reproducing a lot because I've seen many new faces.

By the way, Ninja Nick's black-eye is getting better. As it turns out, I guess Ugly Jen's boyfriend came up to him and was like, "Hey how come your friend Donny won't return my girlfriend's calls?" and Nick was like "Dude, fuck your ugly girlfriend," or whatever and then the dude hit him. **God,** He is gonna fucking get it.

November 16

Here are the results of the First Annual Box of Wine Race at Adam's Sister's House:

1. **Jersey and New York Pete**
2. **Fargo and Bryan**
3. **Me and Ninja Nick**
4. **Adam and his girlfriend**
5 (tie) **Jeff, Kyle Weirdsmelly, Steven, Steve**

Disqualified for not showing up: God, James

It should be noted that all the people who were tied for 5th place never finished their boxes of wine. All in all, I think the First Annual Box of Wine Race at Adam's Sister's House was a success. I mean *I think* it was—I have no recollection of anything that happened after about 10:15 last night.

(Also: must remember get another fetal pig from the lab today because one is missing. I guess somebody either stole or ate one of them?)

November 17

Worked in lab all day after class. Acquired a third fetal pig. Still not sure what happened to missing one? It was right there in the fridge before we went to the Box Wine Race, and when I got back the next morning it was gone. I asked Jersey if he knew what happened to it. He seemed irked that I was storing fetal pigs in his mini-fridge. I made sure to smooth things over by complimenting his calf muscles.

Went out with the guys last night. After a late night at SUNSETS we all decided to crash at Adam's Sister's place. Last night was just good old fashioned fun. Just what I needed after this hard week of studying. Oh-by the way! Madame invited me over to her place for a dinner/study date Sunday night. She's so nice.

Seriously, where the fuck is that pig?

KU CAMPUS POLICE NOTES FOR THE WEEK OF 11/12 – 11/18

Friday, November 16 1:23pm

A student living on Schnellwood Avenue called Campus Police to report a small fire. Two Campus Police officers arrived and discovered a burning orphaned baby pig impaled on a wooden stake in the student's front yard. Officers took care to put out the fire and brought the orphaned baby pig inside the student's house for further examination. A second call to Campus Police was made just minutes later when the officers noticed the pig had not been properly extinguished. A call was then made to the Tomaschevske Fire Department when the pig-fire spread to the walls, floors, and ceilings of the student's home. Officers and resident then evacuated the premises. Tomaschevske Fire Deputies responded to the call quickly and took extreme care to properly extinguish the accidentally-started wall, floor, and ceiling fires, as well as the intentionally-started pig-fire (which by then had all merged into one, very large and very destructive house fire). The student assured Campus Police that he "has a place to stay" while damages are assessed. When asked if he knew who would pig-nap a baby pig, impale it on a wooden stake and burn it to death on his front lawn, the student offered a grim response. He is quoted as saying, "When I find out who is responsible for this I will kill him a hundred times harder than he killed this baby pig." Officers then requested that he stop violently squeezing the charred pig remains so they could preserve it as evidence.

November 17

Just got back to the dorm. Hallway smells really bad. Not bad like *Kyle* bad. More like paint or something. Like some kind of strong cleaning smell. Like somebody sprayed a bunch of Lysol around. But like really, really, really strong, lemon-scented Lysol. It's giving me a headache. Have to go outside and get some fresh air before Thanksgiving Day Week Potluck Feast. I hope Adam and I aren't the only ones wearing pilgrim costumes. Ugh, it smells like toxic gas or something.

Kuhlman University

2900 Salvage Parkway
Tomaschevske, OH 46121

RE: Hallway Cleaning

Donald:

I would like to inform you that you now have a balance of $13.89
with Kulhman University Resident Staff. The charge must be paid in
full before the end of the semester in order to receive your official
grades.

I have detailed the expenses charged to you:

Lemon Fresh Scent RAID	$6.49
X 2 bottles	$12.98
+ tax	$00.91
Total	$13.89

I look forward to dining with you later today at the Thanksgiving
Day Week Potluck Feast in a pest-free environment.

Thank you,

Kenny
ext. 4499

November 17

I cannot believe this. Kenny is such a fucking heartless asshole. How could he do that? He killed off almost the entire colony. I managed to find a few survivors and I took them outside to recuperate. I think the Queen made it to safety just in time. That fucking prick Kenny. He is gonna fucking get it.

KU CAMPUS POLICE NOTES FOR THE WEEK OF 11/12– 11/18

Saturday, November 17 5:43pm

Campus Police responded to a fire call from Montgomery Hall. When officers arrived at the scene they discovered a burning baby pig in front of a Resident Assistant's door. The baby pig had a wooden stake stuck through it. The stake was also burning. Witnesses reported seeing someone dressed as a pilgrim starting the fire. Campus Police suspects that this was an act of protest against the Thanksgiving Day Week Potluck Feast which is held annually in Montgomery Hall. Tomaschevske Fire Deputies, who seemed annoyed that KU Campus Police officers had responded to a fire call, were quick to arrive and to put out the baby pig fire. No arrests were made. Campus Police officers were given extensive literature on fire safety, courtesy of the Tomaschevske Fire Department. The baby pig was pronounced dead at 5:59pm.

November 18

    I need to fucking lay low.

    Have decided to not go on dinner/study date with teacher tonight.

    Hopefully no one makes a big deal about this pig thing.

BABY PIG BARBECUES
Campus Police Cook Student's Home
Maria Bresher, Current Events Editor

Kulhman's campus is no stranger to vandalism, but the occurrences over the last few days have even Campus Policed confused.

Late Thursday evening junior Joseph Ginley looked out his living room window and saw something burning in his front yard. He phoned Campus Police.

Instead of immediately alerting the Tomaschevske Fire Department, Campus Police officers decided to handle the fire themselves. After (partially) extinguishing what they discovered to be a flaming fetal pig carcass, the officers then brought the smoldering creature into Ginley's home. Officers decided to lay the (still hot) fetal pig on a stack of old, dry newspapers to "examine it further." While they were "attending other business" the pig corpse ignited the newspapers and quickly spread to the carpet. Within minutes the entire living room was ablaze.

"I assure you that this house fire was unavoidable," says Officer Jeremy Higley. "There was simply nothing we could do. One minute the pig was on fire, and the next minute he wasn't. And then the next minute after that, he was on fire again. And so was the carpet." When they determined that the fire was not going to "die down on its own" Higley and his partner Officer Greg Baganowski radioed for backup. When two other officers arrived, they knew they had to act quickly. They notified the Tomaschevske Fire Department.

Jason Griggs, one of the firefighters, was disgusted with the way KU Campus Police handled the situation. "You just don't bring a flaming animal into somebody's house. You just don't. What these officers did here was set a house on fire, pure and simple. They put the lives of everyone in that house, and all their neighbors, in danger. For these officers to say that this fire was unavoidable is ludicrous. If anyone is to blame here, it's KU Campus Police."

Officers Higley and Baganowski maintain that the pig was "pretty much not on fire anymore" when they transported into the house.

Campus Police were again on the scene this Sunday when another pig was set ablaze in a residence hall. The Tomaschevske Fire Department was called, and when they arrived they were perturbed that Officers Higley and Baganowski were present.

"If somebody calls Campus Police, that's one thing. But when a person calls the fire department, they want firefighters. They don't want incompetent, so-called police officers showing up and setting their domiciles on fire," says Griggs. "The last thing I wanted to see in that dorm was this pair of idiots. I'm just glad we put the fire out before they had a chance to screw it up and burn down the whole building."

Griggs reminds Kulhman students, faculty and staff to immediately dial 911 – not Campus Police – if they see any sign of a fire.

November 19

Apparently I had quite a celebration after I took third place in the Box of Wine Race. That solves the mystery of the missing pig(s). But I do still have an extra one in Jersey's fridge. That could be incriminating evidence—I need to get rid of it.

I repeat: I need to fucking lay low.

PILGRIMS PASS THE POTATOES
Annual Feast a Success Despite "Protest"
Antoine Regan Levine, Current Events Editor

It's almost Thanksgiving, and that means one thing to the students who live in Kulhman University residence hall: the Annual Thanksgiving Day Week Potluck Feast! Many students gather together during this even to bring foods from their cultures and to share in the holiday spirit.

This year was a slightly different story, however. The Feast, which is held every Saturday before Thanksgiving week, was almost cancelled due to the confusing actions of an on-campus protest group who has yet to be identified by Campus Police.

Before turkey were served, a fire was set in Montgomery Hall, the site of this year's feast. The fire, which was quickly put out by Tomaschevske Firefighters, was caused by a burning dead pig. When asked of the meaning behind such an act of vandalism, one firefighter remarked, "This is the second flaming pig we've seen in two days. I have to believe it's the same person, and that this has nothing to do with a protest of any kind. The fact that this feast was going on must be purely coincidental. I repeat: this was not a protest. There is just some weirdo on this campus who burns pigs. This is clearly related to the pig burning from a few days ago." The firefighter added, "And we also detected a highly unsafe level of pesticide in this dormitory. Breathing this air is like breathing poison. Maybe Campus Police should look into that, and leave the fires to us."

Campus Police has issued a statement describing the pig-burning as "definitely unrelated to any previous pig burnings" and maintains that it "is an obvious act of protest against Thanksgiving" that is "anti-American" in nature.

Hall Director Maya Simari describes Campus Police's statement as "confusing." She explains, "I mean, if you're protesting Thanksgiving, wouldn't you burn a turkey instead of a pig? And wouldn't you leave a note or something? I'm pretty sure this wasn't a protest."

Flaming pigs aside, this Annual Thanksgiving Day Week Potluck Feast went off without a hitch. More turkey, please!

November 19

Here's what I'm thinking: Campus Police
are fucking idiots. They (not me) are the ones
who set Joe's house on fire (by the way, Ninja
Nick is very pleased with the outcome of
"Favor Number 1!"). And it's perfect that
Campus Police think the two pig-burnings have
nothing to do with each other. They're gonna
be out searching for some **Thanksgiving Day
protest group** (do such things exist?). I only
wonder if Kenny is on to me.

Have told the remaining ants that they
should also lay low for a bit until this all
blows over. They are proud of my recent
actions. However, I am not sure if I, myself,
proud.

November 20

I go home for break today. Am catching a
ride with some kid who lives somewhere near
me. His name is Tim or Eric or something like
that. I'll give him gas money. Am taking fetal
pig home with me in case they do room searches
over break. I don't *want* to take it but Jersey
insists (I do not think this has to do with
his being gay).

November 21

Went to Keelie's house. We watched my copy of *Bringing Down the House* starring Queen Latifah and Steve Martin. She dozed off about halfway through the bonus features (I know! I was pissed!). But as I looked at her tiny little head nestled against my chest, and I listened to her peaceful snore, my emotions got the best of me. I thought of how easy life must be for her. She must live day after day without a care in the world. I mean, she fell asleep so easily. She is so guilt-free. So innocent. So completely unconcerned with the fact that the cooler her boyfriend brought over might not just contain sandwiches and an ice pack but is also secretly keeping the body of a fetal pig refrigerated.

Think I am becoming depressed due to the disgusting life I have come to lead and the awful things I have done.

November 22

Thanksgiving. Family. Turkey. Whatever.

November 23

    Just remembered that I had a very important paper for English class due two days ago. I did not write this paper yet. This has made my recently acquired depression slightly more acute.

November 23

    Have decided to type up the paper now. It is a creative writing piece so I should be able to fake it. Maybe writing will ease my feelings of depression.

Hi, Mr. and Mrs. Blake. This is Officer Higley from Kulhman University Campus Police. I hope your family is enjoying some nice holiday togetherness. I wish I were, but I'm stuck in the office over most of break. Somebody's got to be here, you know? If it's not me it's someone else. Eh, it's a rough life but I make ends meet alright. Anyway. I'm sorry to bother you over the holiday like this but I was wondering if either you or your son Donald could give me a call back sometime today? My office extension is nine-nine-two-two. Again, I'm sorry to bother you over the holidays. I will be here in my office until seven this evening. Feel free to call anytime until then. Thanks.

[END OF MESSAGE]

November 23
Fuck. Fuck, fuck, fuck.
Fuck.

104

Transcript of voice message left on home phone of MR. AND MRS. DAVID BLAKE on Friday November 23 at 7:03 PM:

Mr. and Mrs. Blake, this is Officer Higley again calling from Kulhman University Campus Police. I just wanted to try you again before I left for the night. You're probably all out together doing something fun like seeing a movie or getting ice cream. I can't blame you. I know that's what I'd be doing if I still had a family. Eh, it's not your problem, so I won't bore you with the details. Let's just say that this time a year isn't the happiest for me. Anyhoo, I'd appreciate it if you gave me a call back sometime tomorrow. My extension is nine-nine-two-two and I will be in my office, fighting crime remotely, heh heh, until about six in the evening.

[END OF MESSAGE]

November 23

    I don't think I'm going to leave the house all weekend because I have to keep erasing this guy's messages! Doesn't he have anything better to do? Like start more fires? I mean: Doesn't he have anything better to do? Like make more fires *that I started* worse?

    This is the most fucking irked I have ever been in my entire life.

Transcript of voice message left on home phone of MR. AND MRS. DAVID BLAKE on Friday November 23 at 9:15 PM:

Hi, um, I'm not sure if I called the right number. Uh, jeez. Um, this is Jennifer Shapiro. I'm Donny's, uh, I'm a friend of Donny's. From school. From Kulhman. College. I mean University. If he's there could you please have him give me a call back? It is very, very important. Thank you. Goodbye.

    [END OF MESSAGE]

November 23

WHAT THE FUCK?! *WHAT THE FUCK!*

INBOX
From: UGLY JEN
Nov 23, 9:46 PM

DONNY PLEASE CALL ME IT'S IMPORTANT

November 24

    It's 2:57 in the morning. I can not
sleep. I am very confused and worried about my
life right now I think maybe the police want
to arrest me for the pig fires and I will get
thrown out of school and I don't know what
Ugly Jen wants but why does she keep calling
and *why did she call my house* why would she
tell my parents she needs to talk to me this
is so fucked-up I'm just gonna call her back
right now I don't care how late it is what do
I care she called my house for god's sake
maybe she knows why the cops keep calling fuck
I have no idea fuck this sucks.

Transcript of voice message left on mobile phone of DONALD BLAKE on Friday November 23 at 11:43 PM:

Donny. It's Jen. I'm pregnant. It's yours. I know because Joe and I never slept together. Call me back.

November 24

Flipping out. Can't sleep.

OUTBOX
To: NEW YORK PETE
Nov 24, 4:35 AM

HEY PETE ARE YOU AWAKE

November 24

    Am I gonna have to drop out of school?
Oh, wait, I forgot: I'm probably getting
kicked out anyway.

INBOX
From: NEW YORK PETE
Nov 24, 4:41 AM

NO

November 24

    She says she never had sex with her new
boyfriend yet. *Yeah right.* It could be his!

OUTBOX
To: NEW YORK PETE
Nov 24, 4:42 AM

UGLY JEN SAYS I GOT HER PREGNANT

November 24

Maybe she's telling the truth and she really *hasn't* had sex with her new boyfriend and it *is* my kid. Fuck fuck fuck—

INBOX
From: NEW YORK PETE
Nov 24, 4:48 AM

CALL ME TOMORROW IM SLEEPING

November 24

Neither my parents nor Madame Bierbaum-Cardeaux are going to be very happy about this.

OUTBOX
To: NEW YORK PETE
Nov 24, 4:49 AM

WAKE UP I NEED 2 TALK

November 24

And Keelie is definitely never going to have sex with me now.

INBOX
From: NEW YORK PETE
Nov 24, 4:58 AM

NO YOU DON'T. ONLY GIRLS NEED TO TALK AT 4AM. STOP BEING SO FUCKING GAY. FAG.

November 24

This baby is going to be *so ugly*.

November 25

On my way back to school. Not much sleep this weekend. Have kept Keelie in the dark about the whole "I got Ugly Jen pregnant" thing. Think it is for the best, since she is still in the dark about the whole "I cheated on you a bunch with someone named Ugly Jen" thing.

Will write more when I get back to school because the kid I'm getting a ride with (Tim? Eric?) wants to talk for the whole fucking ride. Ech.

November 25

Parents called. Are not happy. Said to call Campus Police.

Transcript of voice message left on office phone of OFFICER JARED HIGLEY on Monday November 26 at 2:13 AM:

Hi, Officer Higley. I guess you're out of your office. I don't know what to say, this is the only chance I had to call you.

Oh, well, I tried, I guess there's nothing else I can do to help you. Good luck with the case!

[END OF MESSAGE]

**Transcript of voice message left on
mobile phone of DONALD BLAKE on Monday
November 25 at 8:05 AM:**

Donny. It's Officer Higley with Campus
Police. I see that you called last night
at...let's see...two in the morning? Nope,
surprisingly I wasn't in the office at
two in the morning on a Sunday night. I
know, weird, huh? I'd like you to stop
by the Campus Police station sometime
this afternoon. Thanks.

[END OF MESSAGE]

November 26

Talked to Officer Higley today. He wanted to know if I knew anything about the recent acts of vandalism involving fetal pigs. I said absolutely not and then he wanted to know how old I was. I said nineteen and he said oh because that's not old enough to go to a bar is it. I said no it's not and he said have you ever been to a place called SUNSETS and I said no. And he pulled out a receipt from SUNSETS with my name on it and he said is this your tab from about November sixteenth for seventeen dollars and I said I wasn't sure and he said this looks like your name and I said yeah I guess it does and he said you didn't leave a tip and I said yeah I usually don't and he said ah-ha so it's yours and I said you got me and he said so you did the pig-burnings and I said no and he said but you just said you got me and I said oh I meant about going to the bar and he said are you sure that's what you meant and I said this is all too much I'm not old enough to be a father and he said what are you talking about and you look kinda pale and then I passed out.

114

November 26

My head hurts. I think I banged it on Officer Higley's desk when I fainted.

Apparently there's going to be some sort of "hearing" or something, for the pig-burnings. Officer Higley says he has evidence and witnesses or something and that if they find out for sure that I did it that I could probably be kicked out of school. But I never admitted to anything! I mean, how could I? I passed out right in the middle of the interrogation. Good thing I have such a weak stomach. Anyway nobody knows about this except me and Officer Higley so far.

November 27

French class was weird today. Madame
wanted to see me after class and asked if
anything was wrong. I played it cool and told
her everything was fine. And as she was
talking, and I was looking at her, I started
to think: *I'm getting kicked out of school and
I got a girl pregnant*. I decided right then to
"bite the bullet" and deal with it all, but
that I would also go down in a blaze of glory
(and explosions). I will no longer play this
stupid back-and-forth game with Madame. I need
to just *get-on her already*.
Enough of this stupid European kissing
bullshit—let's go all the way.

I asked her if she wanted to get
together tonight. She said yes and gave me a
weird look like she was trying to be sexy. It
worked. I mean she is pretty sexy. She doesn't
have to try that hard to be sexy. (Not like
someone like, I don't know, my mom, who would
have to put on like a bunch of make up, and
wear a hot dress, do her hair, you know what I
mean. My mom just doesn't have the natural
sexiness that Madame Bierbaum-Cardeaux has.
Madame is definitely way hotter than my mom.
Not that I think my mom's hot *at all*. That is
not what I'm saying. This is all coming out
the wrong way. A bunch of wrong ways.)

116

November 27

    I am supposed to meet Madame tonight at seven at her place, which is sorta far away.

    Will borrow Ninja Nick's Jeep (I hope he doesn't want any more "favors" because the first one is already getting me kicked out of school).

November 27

    There is a new wrinkle in the plan.

    When Ninja Nick found out what I was borrowing the car for, he went nuts (not *mad* nuts-- *excited* nuts). He said he wanted to cash in his Second Favor. Consequently, Ninja Nick wants to spy (perv) on my date. He reminded me that the other day in the gym I said I would prove that I could get on my teacher. So, the new plan is to try to take Madame back to my dorm (which is now empty and James-less, thank God) and Ninja Nick will be hiding in the closet watching so he can verify to everyone that I did, in fact, hook-up with my teacher.

    I will readily admit that there is an inherent creepy quality to the nature of Ninja Nick's Second Favor, but there's nothing I can do about it. What am I supposed to do? I owe him a Favor. Madame is calling me. I have to go. Wish me luck.

November 28

SOME GOOD THINGS TO REPORT

GOOD: After a few glasses (not boxes) of wine I was able to convince Madame that it would be fun to sneak her into my dorm and spend the night there. I think she thought it would be thrilling/make her feel young again. She would have never done it if I had a roommate. I imagine she also would have declined had she known ahead of time that my small Asian friend would be hiding in the closet watching her every move. Then again, she may have been into it. Who knows.

ALSO GOOD: Instead of being turned off by the décor of my room (which is comprised of a unique blend of dirty laundry, Dave Matthews Band posters and empty plastic liquor bottles) Madame found the style of my living quarters to be fresh, new and captivating. She didn't exactly use those words, though. She didn't exactly use any "real words." She was pretty hammered (from the non-boxed wine). As soon she as she walked in, she sorta just started undressing and mumbling to herself. So I'm kind of *assuming* she liked the look of the room. And I'm also assuming that she wanted to have consensual sex.

118

VERY GOOD: I had sex with my French teacher! Twice!*

*The first time went sort of *quickly*. An encore performance was requested and, after a lengthy intermission, granted.

SOME BAD THINGS TO REPORT

BAD: Ninja Nick watched as I had sex with my French teacher.

ALSO BAD: I'm pretty sure that he, against my very strong personal orders, recorded the whole thing on his video camera (I know, I know—shouldn't he have a digital camera? What's his deal? Does he not know that he's Asian or what?) I kinda wanna put this in the category of good *and* bad. On one hand, the tape is horribly damaging and incriminating. On the other, it's <u>fucking awesome</u>. So I'm torn.

VERY BAD: This morning my newly assigned roommate showed up and saw me laying in bed naked with my French teacher.

THE FUCKING WORST: My newly assigned roommate is Ugly Jen's new boyfriend.

November 29

Ninja Nick and I watched my sex tape about a thousand times.

And then I made him leave so I could watch it by myself. You know what I mean.

Was very careful to a) not show sex tape to Jersey because he is now friend of Ugly Jen's, and b) not show sex tape to Ugly Jen's new boyfriend because he is boyfriend of Ugly Jen's. I just don't want my (potential) Baby Momma to know how much of a scumbag I really am. (Seeing me in bed with a teacher is one thing. Knowing that I had a friend videotape me having sex with her is an entirely different story. Even though I originally didn't know he was going to videotape it-- I just want to reiterate that.)

Oh, by the way, Ugly Jen's new boyfriend—I think I'll just start referring to him as Joe, by the way—has no idea that I had anything to do with the fetal pig incident that almost burned his house down. That is very convenient for me, because as my new roommate, Joe will have tons of opportunities to murder me in my sleep if he wants to. He does, however, know that I may be the father of his new girlfriend's baby. That's going to make our daily hall-mate group workouts a little bit awkward.

120

November 30

I got a letter today from Campus Police and one from the Office of Student Affairs. As much as I love getting mail I'm assuming this isn't the good kind. Haven't opened either envelope yet.

November 30

Opened both envelopes. My hearing is next Tuesday at 7:00pm. That means that I could use this weekend as a nice, relaxing way to get myself recollected and chill out a little bit. You know, take it easy, before things get crazy. Just a *nice, relaxing* weekend. Maybe read a book, plan out my testimony for the hearing. Just something really laid back. I think that would be smart. **Smart** is what I need right now.

November 30

So there I was, sitting in Jersey's room, politely enjoying some of his Cheez-Its, when he happened to open his minifridge. He noticed that my third fetal pig was covertly nestled underneath beneath his Caesar salad from Applebee's (remember—he's gay) and told me how irked he was to see it back in there. I said that I was sorry and that I <u>promise</u> I would get it out of there as soon as I could and that his calves looked great.

Consequently, I have changed mind regarding "nice relaxing weekend" which "would be smart" and decided instead to un-smartly have "drunkest, stupidest weekend of all time." Only because I have to do *something* with this extra pig!

P.S. I think Madame wants to break-up with me or something

P.P.S. This could make French class a little harder. Whatever-- this is my Last Weekend to Party.

Listen up, Ugly Jen. Did you know that we call you Ugly Jen? Huh? Did you know that? Well, now you do. Anyway. Anyways. Whew. I'm spinny. Listen, Jen. Are you listening? It's Donny. You know, your dad. Your dad of your kid, I mean. You know what I mean. Yeah, we had sex. I know that. You don't have to pretend that I don't know what I did and what I didn't do. Who do you think you—

[SOUNDS OF COUGHING]

Sorry. Who do you think you are? You're not my mom. You're maybe my kid's mom. Maybe. But you're not my mom. Hang on.

[SOUNDS OF COUGHING INTERSPERSED WITH SOUNDS OF SPITTING]

Sorry. I keep thinking I'm gonna puke.
Listen, Jen. Ugly Jen. D'you know we
call you that? Did you ever know that
you have a nickname? I bet your new
boyfriend doesn't know—

[SOUNDS OF VIOLENT VOMITING]

[END OF MESSAGE]

Transcript of voice message left on mobile phone of DONALD BLAKE on Friday November 30 at 11:18 PM:

Hi, Donny. This is Jen. Oh, excuse me— you know me as Ugly Jen. I just wanted to thank you for drunk dialing me and puking into the phone. And I also wanted to say that if, in the future, I'm in the exact same room as you, watching a movie with your roommate, you don't have to call me on the phone. I'm directly above you. I can hear you. Oh, god, and I can smell your awful puke.

    [INAUDIBLE]
Ughh, god. Joe, can we sleep in my room tonight?

    [END OF MESSAGE]

December 1

Slamming headache. Have puked many times this morning. "Last weekend to party" is going smoothly. Take that, Kulhman! Will write more later—need to puke again.

December 2

Feel completely awful. Mom called today. Think she could tell I was hungover.
Apparently they invited her and my dad to the hearing on Tuesday. That'll be great.

Need to puke.

December 3

Though I do not remember much of it, I am told that my Last Weekend to Party was a huge success!

PIGMAN STRIKES AGAIN
A Third Pig Burns, Takes Police Station Down with it
Lindsay Blackham, Current Events Co-Editor

Just when Campus Police had assured university officials that the infamous fetal pig vandal was in their clutches, he struck again. At 4:42 Sunday morning, Officer Jared Higley, who was walking up the front steps of the Campus Police Station, discovered what turned out to be a flaming fetal pig impaled on a wooden stake. This is the third such flaming, impaled fetal pig found in the last few weeks.

"I discovered the animal, and then I decided to take action," Higley says. When asked to be more specific, he responded, "It's not my job to be specific. No more questions."

Tomaschevske Fire deputies were called to the scene just a few moments later. They found the entire Campus Police Station ablaze.

Officer Higley maintains that the Police Station fire was "definitively unrelated" to the burning fetal pig.

When asked for comment, Firefighter Jeff Griggs had an emotional response. "This man [Higley] is a complete idiot who deserves to be locked-up. Definitively unrelated? Are you [expletive] kidding me? I mean, are you [expletive] kidding me?! The evidence we, the firefighters, have discovered is completely consistent with what we've seen time and time again with KU Campus Police. The burning pig was not extinguished properly, if at all, and was brought into the station by Officer Higley. Yes. He brought a burning [expletive] animal into the [expletive] police station. Like a [expletive] moron. He started the fire. Forget the pig guy. Arrest Higley."

Regarding both the pig burnings and the allegedly incompetent KU Campus Police Officers, Dr. Robert Siemborski, President of Kulhman University, has stated that he is "confident we will have this whole mess sorted out. There will be swift, unmerciful punishment handed down, one way or another." Siemborski then repeated the phrase "one way or another" and made a menacing fist with his right hand.

December 4

French class was cancelled today. At least I think it was. Madame never showed up, so we all just left. Tonight's the big night. Parents are coming.

The following is a segment from a hearing held by the Office of Student Affairs regarding DONALD BLAKE on the evening of Tuesday December 4. This segment has been transcribed from minutes recorded by Janice Coleman, Assistant Secretary of the Office of Student Affairs:

Dr. Gerald Foyer: Alright, I think everyone's here. Let's get started. I'm gonna be very clear about how this is all going to work. There's very strict procedure we have to follow, of course. First we'll have Officer Higley and myself explain why we're all here, then we'll give each witness a chance to talk, and finally, we'll give Mr. Blake a chance to defend himself. Are we all clear on that? OK. Good. Officer Higley? Why don't you take the floor.

Officer Higley: Thank you, Dr. Foyer.

Dr. Gerald Foyer: Officer Higley, are you okay?

Officer Higley: I'm alright, Dr. Foyer. Just got a few burns from this weekend.

128

Dr. Gerald Foyer: You're on crutches.

Officer Higley: Yeah, I know, it's kinda hard to explain. When the, uh, Police Station started burning, well, I ran out of the building as fast as I could.

Firefighter Griggs: Un-fucking-believable.

Dr. Foyer: Mr. Griggs, please. Watch your language. There are parents here. Go on, Officer Higley.

Officer Higley: As I was saying…you see I was running out of the building, and I ended up tripping over the uh…

Dr. Foyer: The what? What did you trip over?

Firefighter Griggs: He probably tripped over his own fucking feet. The fucking moron.

Dr. Foyer: Mr. Griggs, I will not ask you again. Please refrain from using that type of language and please wait until it is your turn to speak.

Officer Higley: The pig.

Dr. Foyer: I'm sorry?

Officer Higley: I tripped over the pig. The one that was on fire. You see, I had carried the pig into the station to investigate it for clues.

Dr. Foyer: But you put out the fire first, right? I mean you didn't just bring a flaming pig into the Campus Police Station, right? You made sure the fire was out?

Officer Higley: As far as I knew, the fire was out.

Firefighter Griggs: Bullshit!

Officer Higley: The fire was out.

Firefighter Griggs: The fire was not out, you fucking retard!

Dr. Foyer: Mr. Griggs! Take your seat! Mr. Griggs!

Firefighter Griggs: How else did the building start on fire, genius? Huh? How else? You started the fire! Just like you started that kid's house on fire, you fucking idiot!

Dr. Foyer: Mr. Griggs, please wait in the hall. I repeat: step away from Officer Higley and wait in the hall. Mr. Griggs! Officer Higley, are you alright to go on?

Officer Higley: I'm fine, sir. Now, as I was saying, as far as I knew, the pig was no longer burning. And it is my opinion that this man, Mr. Donald Blake, snuck into the Campus Police Station—

Dr. Foyer: After you had put-out the original pig fire?

Officer Higley: Yes. After I had put-out the original pig fire. He snuck in to the station and set the pig on fire again.

Dr. Foyer: You think he waited for you to put-out the fire, waited for you to bring the pig into the station, then snuck into the station behind you and started the pig on fire again without you noticing?

Officer Higley: That seems to be the only possible scenario, in my mind, yes.

Dr. Foyer: Did you *see* Mr. Blake in the Police Station at any time that night?

Officer Higley: Uh, no.

Dr. Foyer: Are you sure there isn't a chance that you only *thought* you put out the pig fire and that it was, in fact, still burning?

December 4

The Hearing took *forever*. I didn't even get to testify yet. This thing is gonna take so long. There's like four other witnesses.

Parents were sorta upset at how long it's going to take. Obviously, they're not staying for the whole thing. They said they would stay in town for a few more days and then go back home. I'm not sure yet if that will be good or bad.

Need to clear my head. Should probably watch my sex tape one more time before bed.

December 5

Had good work-out today. Found out that new roommate (Joe) is pretty strong. We agreed to put the whole drunk-dialing-Ugly-Jen-while-puking thing behind us. After all, us roommates gotta stick together.

My mom wanted to talk to some of the school officials, so I spent the day with my dad. He's not much of a talker.

He's very shy and kinda likes to keep to himself. I don't know if he's taking the whole Hearing thing too well. At one point I was like Dad, what's really on your mind and he started asking me what kinda friends I had, if I was dating any girls, how tall I was getting, if I had any hobbies down at school, that kind of stuff. I figured he was trying to give me some kind of "birds and bees" talk. So I did what I think I was supposed to do: I quickly interrupted and rattled off all the sexual encounters I've ever had as quickly and as detailed as I could. I'm pretty sure that caught him off guard. In a good way. When we met back up with Mom he seemed very happy to see her. Oh well— he's my Dad. But he loves me I think.

December 6

Had parents meet Ugly Jen today. I didn't want that to happen, but when they came to my dorm she just happened to be there, in bed with Joe. They made a big deal about how proud they were I was dating—or had dated—someone my own age.

I was very worried that Ugly Jen would bring up the Ugly Baby subject and that my parents would flip-out but she never mentioned it. Except for the fact that Ugly Jen was in bed with Joe, and pretty much naked and under a blanket the entire time, the whole "meet the parents" thing went pretty smoothly.

I think Joe was sorta irked by the whole thing, though, because Ugly Jen never pointed out that she now dates him. I mean, it was sorta implied, but no one actually came out and said yes, Ugly Jen is now dating Donny's new roommate. Also, there was never any mention of the Hearing, thank God. I made sure of that by just announcing right away, really loudly, that my parents were visiting just for fun and not for any other reason. Then I winked at them so they would get the point. I feel like I have to constantly keep secrets from everybody.

December 7

Got a letter from Office of Student Life. The Hearing will resume on Tuesday. I don't know why they have to make it so dramatic by sending me these letters. Why can't they just call and talk to me instead?

Have decided that since the Hearing resumes on Tuesday, that this is *really* my Last Weekend to Party. For real. Because after next Tuesday I'm probably done for at Kulhman. With that in mind, I think it's a mature, wise and smart decision that I'm making to drink this entire bottle of discount-priced whiskey.

By myself.

Alone in my room.

With the lights off.

And I'll probably put on some George Michael or something.

December 8

Real Last Weekend to Party didn't really start with a bang. I mean, I guess you could say it started with a bang if you consider a few hours of *crying into pillows* and listening to "Last Christmas" by Wham over and over again a bang.

Joe has been giving me the Silent Treatment all day. I don't know what the fuck his problem is.

Transcript of voice message left on mobile phone of JENNIFER SHAPIRO on Friday December 7 at 11:47 PM:

Jen. Hey. It's me. Not Joe. Donny. Your fellow parent. Listen. What's up. Hey. I know, I know, you probably don't wanna hear from me, because I made you meet my parents and we're not even dating and you're dating my roommate and you're probably with him right now talking about how much you love each other and how great and perfect you are together and how you love to kiss and hug and smile and hold each other and--

[SOUND OF MUFFLED WEEPING]

--and how much you just want to spend the rest of your lives together—

[SOUND OF "LAST CHRISTMAS" BY WHAM ENDING AND THEN QUICKLY RESTARTING ON STEREO]

Sorry. I'm sorry to bother you. I
just don't know what to say. It's
gonna be Christmas soon, it's gonna
be cold and you're gonna be cuddling
with Joe in the same room as me and
you guys will be so warm and I'm
gonna freeze to death I just wish I
could crawl into bed with both of you
and just be in the middle of your
Christmas love together and just be
warm and feel you and our baby—

        [SOUND OF VERY SENTIMENTAL, UN-
        MUFFLED WEEPING]

--just the four of us, together—

        [SOUND OF CLIMACTICAL, ANIMAL-
        LIKE SHRIEKING SOBS]

--LAST CHRISTMAS I GAVE JEN MY HEART!
BUT THE VERY NEXT DAY JEN GAVE IT
AWAY! SHE GAVE IT TO JOE!

        [END OF MESSAGE]

December 9

Think I will get Ugly Jen engagement ring for Christmas.

December 11

Had substitute French professor today. Maybe Madame has been sick or something. This one is not very cute, which sucks. Also, this one is a guy, which also sucks.

The big hearing continues tonight. Let's just get it over with already.

The following is a segment from the continuing hearing held by the Office of Student Affairs regarding DONALD BLAKE on the evening of Tuesday December 11. This segment has been transcribed from minutes recorded by Janice Coleman, Assistant Secretary of the Office of Student Affairs:

Dr. Gerald Foyer: Now, Dr. Tolar, you say that you hired Donald Blake to be your assistant in the Biology Lab for the semester?

Dr. Tolar: Yes. That's correct.

Dr. Gerald Foyer: And is Donald a Biology major?

Dr. Tolar: Not to my knowledge.

Dr. Gerald Foyer: Then is he pre-med?

Dr. Tolar: No, Dr. Foyer. He actually made it quite clear on his application, and in several conversations with me since his hiring, that he wanted to pursue either Accounting or Art History as his concentration.

Dr. Gerald Foyer: Did you inform him that Kulhman doesn't offer either of those programs?

Dr. Tolar: Well, no. I mean, he already knew that.

Dr. Gerald Foyer: But he still wants to—

Dr. Tolar: Yes. He's pretty adamant.

Donald Blake: And why *isn't* there an Art History or Accounting program?

Dr. Gerald Foyer: Mr. Blake, this isn't the forum for such a—

Donald Blake: Isn't that what's *really* wrong at this university? Not the pigs, not the fires, not the teachers sleeping with students, not the—

Dr. Gerald Foyer: Teacher sleeping with students? What? Who's doing that? What teachers? Is that what he just said?

Officer Higley: I think that's what he said.

Donald Blake: It's not *any* of those things. The real issue is that there is a serious lack of Art History and Accounting classes at this school. It leaves many students behind, stifling their education and driving them to alcohol--

Firefighter Griggs: I don't see how any of this is relevant. This is a waste of my time.

Dr. Gerald Foyer: Mr. Griggs, please go back into the hallway. We will call you when we need your testimony. Thank you. Now then, Dr. Tolar.

Dr. Tolar: Yes?

Dr. Gerald Foyer: You oversee every aspect of the Biology Lab. Is that correct?

Dr. Tolar: That's fairly correct.

Dr. Gerald Foyer: Fairly? Okay. Does that include the section of the lab that contains the fetal pigs?

Dr. Tolar: Um, yes.

Dr. Gerald Foyer: Did I just sense some hesitation?

Dr. Tolar: Uh, no.

Dr. Gerald Foyer: Did I just sense some more hesitation?

Dr. Tolar: Um, I don't think so.

Dr. Gerald Foyer: Well, do you or don't you?

Dr. Tolar: Are we about finished here?

Dr. Gerald Foyer: What? Finished? No! No-- not even close. Is there something wrong, Dr. Tolar? Uh, Dr. Tolar? Are you okay? Did he just faint? Dr. Tolar? Did you just faint? I think he just passed out. What are we supposed to do? Will somebody go get Mr. Griggs from the hallway?

Officer Higley: If he's a doctor can't he help himself?

Dr. Gerald Foyer: Please just get Mr. Griggs.

Donald Blake: See? This is exactly what I'm talking about! The more we avoid the real issues, the more this kind of stuff happens. If we had an Art History professor up there, he wouldn't pass-out. No way. An Accounting teacher? Please. He'd be *wide* awake.

December 12

They continued the Hearing *again*. So I have to go in next Tuesday, too. Which sucks, because next week is final exam week. Then winter break. And you know what? I couldn't be more ready. I am so sick of Kulhman. I'm sick of my room, I'm sick of my roommate, I'm sick of everybody in this hallway, I'm sick of my classes, I'm sick of not having any ants to play with, and I'm sick of this stupid Hearing bullshit.

December 12

I am not sick of watching my illegal sex tape. I'm thinking of giving it a name. A title or something. Like a sweet porn name. I'll have to do some brainstorming.

December 13

Awful workout today. Saw cute girl in weight room and wanted to talk to her, but when I made my move I started to think about everything going on in my life and I got distracted. I started to think about the baby, and the Hearing and stuff. And then I started thinking about my sex tape and I started wondering if this girl would be the kind of girl that would let me videotape us doing-it. I mean, if we were like dating or something. Or if she wanted to just *not* date me, but do-it with me anyway. And let me tape it. Either way. So, all these thoughts were going through my head and I kinda stepped wrong and tripped on a dumbbell and fell down right in front of her. Then I thought, okay, don't worry, don't worry. If she's really a nice girl she'll help me up. But she didn't notice me, or something, because when I got back to my feet and fixed my sweat-bands and everything she was gone. Just *gone*. Just like everything's gonna be for me pretty soon.

Started looking for cheap engagement
rings online today.

12-14
9:12 PM
FROM: Keelie McNamara@StAnneHighSchool.edu
TO: DONNY MONEY BAGS@hotmail.com

Donny,

I am so excited that you're coming home soon! I can't wait to
see you! I asked for some new movies for Christmas, including
Failure to Launch starring Matthew McConaughey and Sarah
Jessica Parker and *Big Momma's House 2* (which I hear is even
better than *Big Momma's House 1*). We can watch them in my
basement if you want. Good luck with finals. I wish you could
come home this week so I didn't have to wait another seven
days to see you...

Merry Christmas (in advance)
I love you!
Keelie

December 14

Keelie's email has reminded me that this is probably my last weekend ever at Kulhman. With that in mind I have decided to make this my Official Real Last Weekend to Party (For real).

December 14

Have realized that along with being my Official Real Last Weekend to Party (For Real), this weekend is also my Last Chance to Ask Ugly Jen to Marry Me. So, I need to get a ring fast. And I need to distract Joe somehow, so I can have some alone time with Ugly Jen. (I don't feel bad about betraying my roommate, because I became the father of Ugly Jen's unborn Ugly Baby before he moved into my room. So I win.)

December 15

Just as I was getting ready for a full evening of crying and Christmas songs, New York Pete came into my room and invited me to go out with him. He said he didn't want me spending another Friday night alone, partly because we're friends and also partly because I am a loud cryer and I keep him awake at night.

We had a pretty fun time. Kyle (weirdsmelly) came out to SUNSETS with us, as did Adam and his girlfriend. The funniest part of the night was when Fargo and Ninja Nick got into a fight. For some reason or another, those two don't get along with each other anymore. I don't know what caused it, but I turned around at one point to see the two of them rolling around on the floor punching (more like slapping) each other. It was like watching babies fight. It was also funny because the floor at SUNSETS is filthy that when they finally stopped fighting and got up they were covered in grime.

Also, it was my cousin's birthday, which meant that it was my birthday because I have his ID. So, I got a lot of free birthday shots (many of which I gave to Adam's sister to make it look like I was buying her drinks).

All in all, it was just the sort of fun night I needed to help me forget all about my very serious troubles.

December 15

Also, I walked-in on Ugly Jen and Joe having sex today. Man, she *has* packed on some pounds from this Ugly Baby. Sick.

December 15

Joe doesn't know how good he's got it. She's a great lover.

December 15

Adam's sister is having a party tonight. That should be fun. Hopefully I can get Fargo and Ninja Nick to fight each other again. I swear, it was like two crippled puppies trying to softly claw each other to death. I'm sure I can instigate some sort of a disagreement between them and then fuel it with alcohol. That's actually a great idea—because then I can break it up, and look good in front of Adam's sister ("Don't worry—these two guys were fighting in your living room but I took care of it." "Oh, Donny, thank you! Do you want me to have sex with you now?" "You *could* do that, but I don't want your little brother to find out. It might ruin our friendship." "Good point. Then why don't you just have sex with my three hot senior roommates instead? Actually, the hell with it, I'll fuck you, too." "That's a reasonable offer. I accept." Yeah, that's probably how it'll go.)

December 16

I did instigate a fight between Fargo and Ninja Nick, but for some reason it didn't result in group sex with Adam's sister and her roommates. I guess sometimes things don't work out exactly how you plan them.

December 16

I have been studying for like a half hour, almost. This sucks.

December 17

Just finished first two exams. Don't remember what classes they were for but I think I did pretty good on them because I didn't sleep last night because I was studying the whole time.

French exam tomorrow.

Hearing also tomorrow.

Have to take nap.

December 18

French exam was impossible. So fucking hard. I have never even heard of half the shit on that test. I must have failed it. I had to have fucking failed it. Fuck.

Fuck!

What has Madame been teaching me all year?! I thought I was learning things! I went up to the teacher and was like, "Listen, I know you're the new teacher but, dude, I don't know any of this shit, and up until this point, I was doing fine in this class all year." And he was like, "I don't know what to tell you." And then I was like, "Dude. Seriously. What the fuck?"

Fuck.

I'm so irked about this fucking French exam I don't even fucking care about the hearing tonight.

The following is a segment from the
continuing hearing held by the Office of
Student Affairs regarding DONALD BLAKE on
the evening of Tuesday December 18. This
segment has been transcribed from minutes
recorded by Janice Coleman, Assistant
Secretary of the Office of Student
Affairs:

Dr. Gerald Foyer: Mr. Blake, is it correct
that you've been working in the Biology
Lab this semester? That was your on-campus
part-time employment, correct?

Donald Blake: Yes, sir.

Dr. Gerald Foyer: OK. Now, what type
of contact did you have with the large
supply of fetal pigs in the Lab?

Donald Blake: I'm not sure what you
mean by that. What do you mean I had
contact with them? You make it sound
weird.

Dr. Gerald Foyer: What? Listen. Just
answer the question. Did any of your
duties as a Lab Assistant require you
to deal with the fetal pigs or move
them around? Dr. Tolar informed us
that some of your duties involved
putting away the fetal pigs. Is that
true?

Donald Blake: Oh, I think I
misunderstood the question--

Dr. Tolar: I never said that.

Dr. Gerald Foyer: Excuse me?

Dr. Tolar: I never said that.

De. Gerald Foyer: You never said what?

Dr. Tolar: I never said anything. *I don't even know this kid.*

Dr. Gerald Foyer: Dr. Tolar, what do you mean? Of course you know him. This is Donald Blake, the freshman. You hired him. You two worked together in the Biology Lab. He was your assistant.

Donald Blake: Yeah, it's me. Donny. What is wrong with you?

Dr. Tolar: I swear--*I don't know him*!

Dr. Gerald Foyer: I really don't understand this. Dr. Tolar, didn't you hire Donald Blake to be your assistant for the semester? I thought this was all pretty clear.

Officer Higley: I'm positive I've seen those two together on campus.

Firefighter Griggs: Yeah, even I've definitely seen them together and I don't work here. I'm with idiot cop on this one. Dr. Tolar must be lying.

Officer Higley: Thanks, Griggs. Dr. Tolar, why don't you just admit that you know him? What's the big deal?

Donald Blake: Yeah! Tell them, Dr. Tolar! Tell them you know me!

Dr. Gerald Foyer: Dr. Tolar! Do you or don't you know this student?!

Dr. Tolar: You've got the wrong guy! I don't know him! *I swear I don't know him! Ahhhh!*

Firefighter Griggs: Was that lightning outside?

Dr. Gerald Foyer: Where did he go? Uh, okay. Hmm. Um, let's see. Okay. Let's…um. Hmm. Please let the record show that when questioned about his relationship with Donald Blake, Dr. Peter Tolar denied knowing him three times. And then he ran from the room screaming. Is that about right?

Firefighter Griggs: And then lightning struck.

Dr. Gerald Foyer: Yes, of course. And then lightning struck.

Firefighter Griggs: I'm gonna go outside and check that out.

Dr. Gerald Foyer: Can someone find Dr. Tolar? I'm *sure* we have to ask him some more questions. I mean, don't you think we should?

Officer Higley: Why? Was he acting weird or something?

December 18

They decided to give Dr. Tolar his own personal Hearing. Or trial. Whatever the fuck it is. I guess he creeped everyone out enough. What the fuck is that guy's problem? Public speaking must make him nervous or something.

Anyway, since it's finals week and they can't continue the Hearing next Tuesday ('cuz it's Winter Break) I have to go back tomorrow night. Hopefully it's the last fucking time because I have so much fucking studying to do.

On the bright side, there was that thunderstorm tonight that started during the Hearing. Some of the ants decided to come in to my room to keep dry. It was nice to see some old friends.

The ants and I tried getting some Cheez-Its from Jersey but they're all gone. All of them! Can you believe it?

He said that Fat Ugly Jen has just been *devouring* everything in his closet lately. And trust me, it shows. She is fucking *huge*. God, that Ugly Baby sure has an appetite. I wonder if it's a boy? I hope my son isn't born addicted to Cheez-Its.

Donald Blake
209 Montgomery Hall
DONNY MONEY BAGS@hotmail.com

RE: Not kicking me out of school

Dr. Foyer and the Office of Student Life:

      I want to take this opportunity to first say what a pleasure it has been coming to these meetings with all of you. Though it is a shame that our time together must undoubtedly come to an end, rest assured that I won't ever forget these soon-to-be cherished memories. The moments we spend with those we love and cherish are those that matter most in life. I blush to admit that you, the members of the Office of Student Life, have become dear to me, though we've only known each other for a brief time. I look forward to developing our relationships together in my upcoming semesters at Kulhman (as long as you don't vote to expel me).

      I also want to make it clear that this statement is not meant in any way to *influence your decision* regarding my expulsion. After all, that choice is yours to make. I only implore you to listen to all of the witnesses' stories and carefully weigh your decision with Kulhman University's best interests in mind. If, at the end of your investigation, if it becomes clear to you that this rich and tremendous university campus would function better without my presence, then, by all means, *give me the boot*. Really, I'm not trying to sway your decision (not at all!) This is more of a friendly letter. Like a formal "Hello."

Hello!

With that innocent disclaimer in mind, I would like to say a few things about myself. First, I am a proud student of Kulhman University. Ever since I received my acceptance letter just a few short months ago I have felt a blossoming joy deep within my torso that has only expanded over this semester. It has expanded much like a balloon expands when one inflates it with air. Yes, my torso has turned into a virtual balloon of joy because of my time here at Kulhman University. And I sure would hate to have that torso-balloon popped. But again, that decision if yours to make.

As you all know (or can imagine in great and colorful detail) college life is full of surprises. And I mean surprises! My first semester here has been wrought with success, failure, friendship, hardship, bank fraud and pregnancy (both the bank fraud and the pregnancy were accidental). All of those things have led to my personal, academic and [find other adjective] growth. I must admit, all this growth I've experienced might go right out the window if I get kicked out of school (which would be a real shame). But don't worry about me—I trust you'll make the right decision either way.

When I moved in to Montgomery Hall, I found myself living with a loving, caring, and compassionate roommate who I will call James. We became best friends right off the "bat" (if you lived in Montgomery Hall you would get the joke). But ever since he mysteriously disappeared I have had a hard time dealing with college life. With no one's strong, reassuring shoulder to cry on, college life can sometimes be intimidating. And lonely. Really lonely.

And that is why I stole and set fire to three fetal pigs. Please find it in your hearts to forgive me and to let us all move on with our rich and tremendous lives. I just have one more thing to say. You guys should really look into adding an Art History and Accounting majors. If Kulhman wishes to remain a competitive liberal arts university it is going to have to start changing with the times. Both Art History and Accounting are two of the most popular areas of study at many leading universities*. I look forward to majoring in either one or both of those programs during my upcoming semesters at Kulhman.

Respectfully yours,
Donald Blake

*The popularity of either Art History or Accounting at any university or college has not been formally researched or verified by the author of this statement.

The following is a segment from the continuing hearing held by the Office of Student Affairs regarding DONALD BLAKE on the evening of Tuesday December 19. This segment has been transcribed from minutes recorded by Janice Coleman, Assistant Secretary of the Office of Student Affairs:

Dr. Gerald Foyer: Mr. Blake, were you aware of any records kept by Dr. Tolar regarding the amount of fetal pigs that came in and out of the lab?

Donald Blake: I thought this hearing was about me.

Dr. Gerald Foyer: Mr. Blake. Please answer the question. Did Dr. Tolar keep detailed records of any kind regarding the fetal pigs?

Donald Blake: I honestly have no idea. I never saw any, if he did. Why? Who cares?

Dr. Gerald Foyer: Do you even know *where* the pigs came from?

Donald Blake: No. All I know is that when they came in, I had to put them in the big coolers.

Dr. Gerald Foyer: Did the boxes they came in have any address or anything on them?

Donald Blake: I'm not sure. I don't think so. Now that I think about it, the shipments were kind of secretive and weird. Dr. Tolar would act sorta of odd whenever new fetal pigs came in.

Dr. Gerald Foyer: Sorta odd? What do you mean?

Donald Blake: Uh, let's see. He would kinda lock the place down, like turn off all the lights and lock all the doors. He would make me turn my cell phone off. I always thought that was pretty weird. Like it was a big drug deal or something.

Dr. Gerald Foyer: I see. That certainly does seem strange. And about how many pigs would come in a shipment, would you say?

Donald Blake: Oh, god. Way too many. Just way more than the school needs, I'm sure. If I would ever ask Dr. Tolar how many there were, he'd get cranky.

Dr. Gerald Foyer: Cranky?

Donald Blake: Yeah. Like one time, I think the last time I was helping him stock a shipment, I said hey Dr. Tolar, this is a lot of pigs, you know, how many pigs are there? And he just snapped at me. He said it was none of my business and that it wasn't my job to count the fetal pigs and that I should shut my stupid mouth and put the pigs in the cooler and mind my own fucking business. You know, just cranky.

Dr. Gerald Foyer: Mr. Blake, please watch your language.

Donald Blake: I only said fucking because he said fucking. I was just repeating what he said to me. Sorry.

Dr. Gerald Foyer: It's fine. Mr. Blake, did you ever think about telling anyone about Dr. Tolar's odd behavior?

Donald Blake: Well, as I pointed out before, I don't plan on majoring in science or anything, so I figured who cares. I actually plan on majoring in either Art History or Account—

Dr. Gerald Foyer: We know.

Donald Blake: Listen. Dr. Foyer. Can I just be straight with you?

Dr. Gerald Foyer: I insist.

Donald Blake: Okay. Listen. It's finals week. I have a lot of studying to do. Can we please just get this over with? Look, can I just pass out this statement I prepared? I made enough copies for everyone.

Dr. Gerald Foyer: Mr. Blake, I'm sure you understand we have strict procedure—

Donald Blake: *Yes*, I set a pig on fire outside some kid's house. *Yes*, I set a pig on fire outside my RA's door while dressed as a pilgrim. *Yes*, I set a pig on fire outside the Campus Police station. And *yes*, I'm mostly sorry about all of those things. Look, I don't know about Dr. Tolar's weird fetal pig operation he has going on, and I honestly don't care. I took the lab job because it was easy and I needed some money. Dr. Tolar is weird and he orders tons of fetal pigs. There. That's it. I don't know what else I can tell you. Except that my fucking ugly ex-girlfriend is pregnant, *and* really fat, and I really have to study for my final exam in American History and I still need to go over a lot of dates for the multiple choice section and this hearing has gone on way too fucking long and if you're gonna kick me out of school at least just tell me now so I can know if I have to go read about the American Revolution or not.

Dr. Gerald Foyer: Look, everyone, why don't we take a ten minute recess—

Mme Cardeaux: You cannot expel that student!

Dr. Gerald Foyer: Um, we weren't going to.

Donald Blake: You weren't?

Dr. Gerald Foyer: Who is that?

Officer Higley: Ma'am, I'm gonna have to ask you to wait outside. This is a closed hearing.

Mme Cardeaux: Monsieur Donald Blake has a heart of gold!

Officer Higley: What is she, Spanish or something?

Firefighter Griggs: She's French, retard.

Donald Blake: Yeah, she's French.

Dr. Gerald Foyer: Miss, who are you and what business, if any, do you have here?

Mme Cardeaux: Je suis le professeur de français!

Dr. Gerald Foyer: What does that mean?

Donald Blake: She's my French professor. She's sort of obsessed with me.

Dr. Gerald Foyer: Okay?

Officer Higley: It looks like she was Mr. Blake's reference, on his application to work at the Biology Lab. Here, take a look.

Dr. Gerald Foyer: Okay, but what does that—hey! Are you two kissing? Are they kissing? Whoah! Stop! Stop that, whatever you're doing! Hey! Stop it!

Firefighter Griggs: Oh, that is so fucking hot.

Mme Cardeaux: Donny, ooh. Oh, I have missed you.

Officer Higley: Um, Dr. Foyer? Uh, don't you want me to kick her out of here? This is…highly inappropriate. Like really bad.

Firefighter Griggs: Let the kid have some fun before he gets expelled.

Dr. Gerald Foyer: He's not getting expelled!

Donald Blake: Really? Madame, hang on a second. Seriously, hold on. Am I really not getting expelled?

Officer Higley: Let's go, break it up. Come on. Miss, come on. You'll have to wait in the hallway.

Mme Cardeaux: Oh, Donny! Mon chère! I will do anything I can to help you!

Donald Blake: Madame, I have something to tell you. You might not be too happy about it.

Mme Cardeaux: Whatever it is, Donny, it will not stop the raging passion I have for you!

Officer Higley: Let's go! Out the door!

Donald Blake: I got some other chick pregnant.

Mme Cardeaux: Oh, mon dieux! That is bad. But do not worry, mon chère. We will find a way to make things work! I want to be with you!

Officer Higley: Let's go, lady! Outside!

Dr. Gerald Foyer: Alright. Let's all take a break. We will meet back here in ten minutes and hopefully finish this thing up. I need to get some air.

Firefighter Griggs: Hey, kid. I would kill to have a hot French chick like that all over me. Nice work.

Donald Blake: Yeah, I guess. But I don't know if I wanna be with her the way she wants to be with me. I mean, it's cool, you know, to be able to say, yeah, I did-it with my French teacher. But after that, it's like, echh. I'm nineteen. I'm not gonna date some chick who's forty-four. No way, you know?

Firefighter Griggs: Yeah, I could see that. You're young. But still. I mean, jeez.

Donald Blake: She just got really attached to me.

Firefighter Griggs: I think you have like three hickeys on your neck already.

Donald Blake: That's nothing. You should see what else she does.

Firefighter Griggs: I only wish, kid. I only wish.

Donald Blake: Hmm. If you want, I could give you a copy of *The Da Donny Code*.

Firefighter Griggs: You mean *The Da Vinci Code*?

Donald Blake: Close. *The Da Donny Code* is the sex tape I made with Madame Bierbaum-Cardeaux. I think I have a copy in my bag.

Firefighter Griggs: Is there a mysterious plot with ancient puzzles and clues and stuff?

Donald Blake: Uh, kinda. It's pretty much me having sex with my teacher, with scenes from the actual *The Da Vinci Code* movie crudely edited in here and there. Here ya go.

Firefighter Griggs: You sure you wanna give me this?

Donald Blake: Yeah, yeah, go ahead. I have tons of copies. It's not bad considering it was shot from inside a closet. Hey, wait. Is *she* getting all this? Ms. Coleman? Are you typing everything I'm saying? You are? Seriously? Fuuuuuuuuck.

December 19

The stupid fucking Hearing is finally over. Thank god. I don't think I'm getting kicked out of school. But I think Madame Bierbaum-Cardeaux is. That's probably for the best.

I'll write more tomorrow. I have to study for this stupid fucking American History exam. Peace.

December 20

I feel pretty good about the History test. One of the essays gave me some trouble but I'm pretty sure I schmoozed my way through it.

Whew. One semester of college down. Congratulations, self! (Thanks, self! Congratulations to you, too!)

In other news, roommate Joe seems bummed out about something. (Maybe he knows that I'm going to propose to his girlfriend Fat Ugly Jen? Sucker!)

December 20

If I have time later, I want to try to put *The Da Donny Code* up on YouTube.

AMERICAN HISTORY HIST 101-02

NAME: Donald Blake

STUDENT ID#: 000154263

ESSAY 2:

Please explain the significance of four events that impacted the outcome of the Revolutionary War. Be specific (names, dates, etc)!

Like many other Americans, I find war to be a tragic and sad aspect of life. It is tragic that we have all this freedom and all these rights and we throw it all away to shoot at one another and use violent force. And it is sad because war can often tear apart families and houses. As well as marriages.

But to answer your question, the "Revolutionary War", which was fought several decades ago, had many events that impacted it. Many events. Many significant events. It would fill an entire book if we tried to list and explain the many significant, impactful events. Suffice it to say that it was Vietnam all over again. Which is, again, both tragic and sad.

War is always a mistake. That's one thing I've learned from this class. I'm sure you agree that the Revolutionary War was no exception. That war should never have happened. So many lives were lost and so many un-lost lives were injured. I hope we have learned some wisdom from our ancient American ancestors and we will never fight a war again. One was enough (more than enough).

I hope you have enjoyed grading my final exam as much as I enjoyed taking it. I wish you and your family a nice, relaxing winter break. See you next semester. As long as I don't get kicked out of Kuhlman sometime before then. It's a long story; don't ask.

-Donny ;)

December 21

To tell the truth, I was kinda looking forward to getting kicked out of school. Deep down I think I was okay with it. I mean, with this Ugly Baby on the way, I have to get a real job. Getting expelled would have been an easy way for me to be like, listen, Mom and Dad, I have to get a job to support this new Ugly Family of mine. Oh, well. I guess I'll be at Kulhman for at least another semester.

Alright, I gotta go. I'm gonna find Ugly Jen and ask her to marry me. I'm not even nervous. With all I've been through lately, this will be *nothing*. I wonder if Kulhman will let us live together in the same dorm, since we'll be a family? Doesn't matter—I'll figure out the details later.

Wish me luck!

December 21

I went over to Ugly Jen's place to propose to her and she was crying when I walked in. I asked what was wrong and she showed me a pregnancy test (which *I didn't touch*, by the way, because I think it was probably covered in her gross piss). The test showed that she *wasn't pregnant*. I asked her why she was so convinced that she was pregnant all this time and she said it that at first she wasn't sure but she was pretty sure, and then when she started gaining all the weight she was convinced.

Are you fucking kidding me!

So this whole time I think that Ugly fucking Jen is fucking pregnant and it turns out she's *just fat*?!

MOTHER-*FUCKER*!

Anyway, so she asked me why I came over in the first place, and I said I definitely *didn't* come over to ask you to marry me, you stupid fucking idiot. Then I stormed out and slammed the door behind me.

December 21

    Then I reopened the door, stormed back in and had sex with Un-pregnant Ugly Jen.

December 22

    *Now that I think about it, more sex may not have been the best way to celebrate an un-pregnancy.

December 22

    MUST START MAKING BETTER DECISIONS.

WEIRDO BIO PROFESSOR RELEASED
Underground Fetal Pig Scheme Exposed
Paula Garvey, Staff Reporter

Kulhman University has finally made a decision regarding the recent acts of vandalism involving the on-campus burnings of fetal pig specimens. After lengthy proceedings headed by the Office of Student Affairs, Dr. Gerald Foyer has discovered the guilty party: a student at Kulhman University.

However, according to the Office of Student Affairs, the student will not be expelled, or punished in any way. The student, whose name Dr. Foyer refuses to make public, has been instrumental in unraveling a mysterious black market crime ring that has been operating on Kuhlman's campus for the past several months.

Dr. Peter Tolar, who was until recently the Senior General Manager of the Biology Lab, was terminated and turned over to federal investigators. Tolar faces what interviewed federal agents have referred to as "very serious and very disgusting" charges.

Campus Police Officer Jared Higley maintains that he "knew all about Tolar the whole time" and that the headstrong investigation of the unnamed student vandal allegedly involved in the on-campus burnings was "simply a roundabout way to get to Tolar and this black market pig business."

In response to Higley's claim that the student vandal was used as bait to catch Dr. Tolar, local firefighter Jason Griggs had this to say: "Officer Higley is so [expletive] full of [expletive]. He had no idea about this black market pig thing. Let me ask you a question. Does he look smart to you? Does he? Seriously, I want you to tell me. Look at him. Go ahead, take a look. Does he look like a bright guy to you? Didn't think so. Case closed."

All that is known so far about Dr. Tolar's operation is that it involved receiving large shipments of fetal pigs from non-sanctioned laboratories somewhere in Norway. Tolar stored the specimens on KU's campus, in the Biology Lab coolers. Instead of using the specimens for classroom exercises, Tolar illegally resold them to underground laboratories in Southern and Northeastern Ohio.

Investigators do not yet know the nature of what exactly it is these other, criminally operated labs were doing with the pigs.

"We'll find out. We always do," Federal Agent Beven Kahler confidently declared. "Everyone thought Dr. Tolar was your average weirdo bio prof, and that some punk kid was stealing pigs from him and setting them on fire for kicks. It appears that what this, quote, punk kid was really doing was making a statement against Dr. Tolar's actions. What this punk kid did in burning these pigs was rebel against a federal crime and the exploitation of animals all over the world. Punk kid? Hardly. He's a hero."

Tolar has reportedly been involved in this fetal pig scheme since February. He could not be reached for comment.

ATTRACTIVE FRENCH PROFESSOR RELEASED
Interrupts Meeting, Declares Love for Student
Sheila McGrath, Staff Reporter

During a private hearing in the Office of Student Affairs this Wednesday evening, Professor Bierbaum-Cardeaux made a startling announcement.

Bierbaum-Cardeaux reportedly burst into the room and, in a thick French accent, declared her love for a male undergrad.

Dr. Gerald Foyer, Dean of Student Affairs, was quite shocked by the woman's interruption. Foyer remarked that he "was quite shocked by the woman's interruption. And I was also shocked by how smooth her legs looked. I mean, the lighting in the room is pretty standard, but for some reason her thighs were just…well, simply put, her thighs were shimmering. And remarkable."

Following her announcement, the busty French professor allegedly mounted the object of her affection, an unnamed male undergrad, and smothered him with kisses and sincere affection. Secretary of Student Affairs Janice Coleman described the display as "completely inappropriate for a professor." Coleman continued to say, "This woman is a disgrace to every French immigrant who has ever come to America to teach the French language to American college students. Her only saving grace is that her legs are exceptionally smooth and shiny for someone her age. They also have a subtle hint of essence of mango. When she rushed past me on her way to molest the student I thought I was in a lush mango orchard in some foreign land in the middle of July."

Bierbaum-Cardeaux was terminated the following day. When asked whether or not she plans to continue her relationship with the student she responded in French. Though a translation of her response could not be obtained, this reporter thought her unintelligible words to be passionate and engaging, and that her legs did, in fact, possess a slight mango scent.

Kuhlman University

Office of Admissions
2900 Salvage Parkway
Tomaschevske, OH 46121

Parents and Families,

We at the Kulhman University Office of Admissions Staff
hope you found the Holiday Season a warm and joyous
one. Our students certainly earned their Winter Break.
While we plan to enjoy the time off as much as they will,
we look forward to the start of another semester in just
a few weeks.

As many of you know, there has been quite a demand
for change at Kulhman. During this semester the
current course and degree listing has been criticized by
students and applicants for not being "relevant" or "up-
to-date" enough. Although Kulhman prides itself as the
famed "Glove-Box of the Midwest," its diversity has
recently been called into question. A main concern is
that Kulhman doesn't provide certain degrees that other,
bigger universities offer. Two programs in particular
were specifically mentioned time and time again to
faculty and staff. Critics have insisted that if these two
missing programs were added to Kulhman's course and
major listing, it would be an even more complete
university.

One of the qualities that makes Kulhman University's
staff so unique is its willingness to listen to criticism. We
are well aware that the academic world (and beyond) is
one of constant change. Kulhman University is ready to
change and to grow along with its student body (and
with the rest of the academic universe at large).

With that in mind we are proud to announce that Kulhman has decided to open *two new, fully-staffed departments*. These two new departments will offer over thirty new undergraduate courses and two new undergraduate degrees. We hope that those members of the student body who have voiced their opinions so fervently will be satisfied that their pleas have been answered. Starting Fall Semester, Kulhman University will now offer both **Respiratory Therapy** and **Women's Studies** as the two newest undergraduate degree programs.

No other programs are slated to be added to Kuhlman's current listing.

Sincerely,

Alice Closser,

Kulhman University Office of Admissions

CPSIA information can be obtained at www.ICGtesting.com
Printed in the USA
LVOW101405270712

291862LV00001B/53/P